THE CLASH OF TRIBAL LINES

By Shanck Weberson

Clash of Tribal Lines
ISBN: 978-1-7346538-4-7

Abomination in the Family
ISBN: 978-1-7346538-0-9

Seasonal Work Journey
ISBN: 978-1-7346538-2-3

Chapters

Kidnappings and Deaths

Run quickly Amman! Adaku said. She turned left and right and left again, just to be sure. Adaku prayed in her heart that this night is not their turn to be taken. But why has she come this far? The instruction was to stay on the edge of the forest; not to go into it. After the first 'Takings' were reported, a message was passed around to avoid the forest and beyond. Hunting would be left to experienced and brave warriors who would venture into the forest and bring back whatever was needed. That would be shared amongst all households according to the number of persons who lived in them.

Adaku said a prayer and hoped a god might be idle tonight and come to her rescue. Amman joined her at the base of the Bristlecone pine. Its base has projections like bare branches from its trunk that ran to the ground and formed a wall that separates the trunk of the tree from the others. This created a small enclosure, giving them a hiding place, and protection if the monster was watching them from a tree, waiting for the right moment.

The howling sound came again. Amman shook like someone with a fever. He held Adaku so tight, she felt some pain. Adaku had to plan the next move, find a way out of this forest and get home before her mama notices that she is missing. They sprint across the clearing into a wooded patch. This area seemed safer than the other side of the forest. They held hands together and stalked among the trees staying close to every tree trunk to avoid being seen.

Adaku closed her eyes and, in her mind, tried to remember what part of the forest they were and how best to exit the forest. Their best bet was to follow the stream. This would lead them to open land and onto the town farmstead and they would be free. Adaku drew Amman up, walked towards the stream. Adaku thought of swimming to fasten their escape but knowing that Amman was not a good swimmer. The walk along the side of the stream was quiet except for the sounds from the water as it rolled upon the stones. The moonlight on the stream made it shimmer, it was serene all around. In another life, this could have been where she wanted to stay; the trees and birds in the day and the moonlight on the stream at night. Adaku shook the thought out of her head. This was not the night, it was a matter of life and death now. The faster they made it out of this forest, the safer it was for Amman and herself. Wildflowers grew out from the banks of the stream, she could not tell the colors of all of them, but she could smell the scent they gave out. The stream took a bend and flowed beside a small clearing where Bloodroot grew from rocks.

It came with the sound like a whisper. She only felt her hair brush against her skin. Adaku turned around and Amman was gone. Fear gripped her and she ran with all her might. She sobbed as she ran. This was all her fault. Adaku had begged Amman to come with her and promised to be his mate during the Harvest festival dance. All Adaku had wanted, was for him to accompany her to the forest to get some Mornadella, to make a beauty potion so that she could win at the May Queen contest. She never really liked Amman; she agreed to go with him to the dance because no other boy had asked. She wept copious tears as she ran.

Adaku came to open land where the stream diverted to the sea. Adaku made to run across it, but it was there waiting for her. Its ferocious teeth glistening in the moonlight, its powerful limbs, its red fur, and those evil eyes. This was the end. With one swipe of its arm, it went for Adaku neck.

The next disappearance happened the day of the annual pilgrimage. The annual pilgrimage to the shrine of Freya, the goddess of fertility is filled with anticipation. This time, Abeo would make sure to participate in the rituals. Abeo had brought along with him two cows and some lambs for sacrifice. It has been ten years since he had married Ava and no child has come. Ten years he watched as his brothers and friends bore children and become full members of the clan. It seemed Abeo luck was not for good. Abeo wants to go and ask Freya to bless his wife with a child or ask her for a second wife. After all, what do you call a man without a child, without an heir to carry on his name? He would speak with the priests of the shrine and meet with the seer. This is too be Abeo's last chance to receive a heir or he would not come back.

Climbing the little hill seemed difficult for the horse. It took a lot longer to make progress. This delay distracted Abeo from his thoughts, he began to get angry but noticed the quick movements of something in the trees. The horse neighed again and stopped. This time, it showed signs of fear. He jumped down from the horse and unsheathed his sword, scanning the tree canopy. Time passed and nothing happened. He walked his animals, this time gently, watching the tree branches above for any sign of movements. Abeo had heard rumors of the monster that took travelers on this route. This would not deter him from making this all-important journey. More than anything, this journey was about honor and pride. It was about the survival of his name. This was not Abeo time to die. No, it is never going to be his time.

In one mighty sweep of the hand, it took him, the horse neighed, the other animals ran away. There was no cloth, no marks, no body, and no trace. That was the last time Abeo was seen.

The Meeting

The meeting was called in the Hall of Gathering. The men came in one by one wearing long stony faces. They filled the room, at the doorways were elves, some carrying coats, others taking the horses. The heads of households have gathered to deliberate. It is an all-important function to safeguard the tribe, a function that reigns supreme above every tribal law.

The Hall of Gathering is a large tent-like erection. It is made of wood, animal skins and cloth. The wood is used to make the base and serve as a foundation for the tent, the walls, doors, and other fixtures. Then a large cloth is used to make the roof. Animal skins is put under the cloth on the top of the Hall to conserve heat. In this Hall, the chief meets with all the Heads of Houses of the tribe. On some occasions, all men were asked to assemble here. It is located in the center of the town and is a sign of unity, a bond of the tribal feel.

It had rained all night and a mist had descended on the village bringing with it cold. In the center of the room is a small fireplace, over the entrances are hung protection charms to keep evil away. Everyone, as well as the chief, sat on stools; symbolizing the equal-ness of every man in the tribe. The large gray beard on his chin seems to feel the mood of the room and doesn't wriggle in all directions as it was wont to do. Instead each strand seemed to stay with one another as though trying to comfort themselves.

In a husky voice, the ruler of this tribe began. "My brothers, a great cloud has fallen upon us, the winds have turned its tide against us. We have heard reports of missing children, women and men. A monster now lives among us. He leaves his victims without heads when he has killed them, and taken some without a trace left behind.. Our people have become filled with fear, we now prefer to stay indoors, than go about our occupations. We have now become a people of fear. This is not us. This is not our legacy but here we are because we have lost some of our people to a monster that is ravaging our countryside. The strength of our tribe is in the survival of every man, woman and child. Our survival is dependent on our strength. It is time for us to act or face an uncertain future and certain destruction of tribes'. At the mention of this, the men shook their heads and murmured. The chief continued, "We must act now to stop this menace; for our future, for our tribe". A hush fell over the Hall. All seemed to be engrossed in their own thoughts.

Eddard, an elder of the clan, rises from his seat and speaks his mind. He begins, "My brothers, my mother's sons, we must not be ruled by fear. Rather, let us march into the forest, with axes and swords and hunt this monster down. We are children of the moon, we shall be victorious. Didn't the Northmen attack us? Didn't we defeat them and plundered their armies? Have we not been hunted by the Zorostars, that race of wizards? We cut their magic, destroyed their race. We made them pay for every life that was lost. Fear and sadness has never been known to us, it will not be known to us in our time. Aye!" Many men pounded their staffs on the wooden floor of the Hall, to acknowledge what Eddard had said.

Elder Reni stood up. "It has been a part of our history to meet great evils from time to time. Our ancestors have always faced it headlong and we have been victorious. I say we take what good Eddard has said and march into the forest to hunt down this monster. Aye!"

After a lot of chants and speeches in support of Elder Eddard's proposition, Elder Kent was next. "My brothers, my mother's sons. Today we have shown that we have not been quick to forget history and all the great achievements of our tribe. However, it is important that we tread carefully in this matter. An invasion of a tribe is not the same as the sudden appearance of magical creatures. The recent happenings have shown that something sinister is at play in our village".

Wolzart, the Iron bender, raised up his head and said: "pray, tell us what you mean by those words". "We need to seek the seer's words on this". Elder Kent continued; we need to pay a visit to the Temple of Wisdom. The victims whose bodies we have seen always come with their heads broken and empty like a broken water pot. We all know of one monster capable of leaving its victims this way. We know that the appearance of the Nandi Bears represents a coming disaster. Doom. Only a few weeks before the recent incidents, some hunters in the Uzars, our neighboring clan, said that they spotted Bokwus in the hinter region. My brothers, mother's sons, it is time to get battle-ready, I agree. It is of paramount importance to find out what kind of battle we are going into". Wolzart sat down.

There was no pounding of staffs or chants or applause. It was the words of the chief that ended the gathering. It was time to see the Seer, after all these years. It was time. He named names; gave a day to set out to the Temple of Wisdom. The elves brought out their coats and all the men returned to their homes.

The Clash of Tribal Lines

The Prophecy of Sibylla

The journey to the temple was a days journey. The temple was on a rocky mountain. It was not difficult to ascend and afforded people of all ages to ascend it. The site has remained a revered site since ancient times. People from every land came to this shrine. It was said that at the End of Days, when all will be destroyed and the sun has been eaten by the god of darkness, the gods will descend on this holy site and live there. This place will see no destruction.

The roads leading up to the mountain were paved with rocks and stones. There were flowers in some corners and none in other parts. This is the only place where flowers can be found all year round in full bloom. It was forbidden to take any, calamity has said to have befallen those who did not obey. At every corner along the path, in little grottoes, a priest leads a small congregation of pilgrims in prayers and counseling. The priests were lightly dressed in dark robes revealing most of their arms and had shaved heads. A first glance at them would make a first-timer feel safe. They had a warm and welcoming countenance, smiling whenever they had the chance to. On their heads were tattoos describing different marks representing the rank of each priest. There are 13 ranks in all and it takes years to ascend to the last rank of priesthood.

The Chief, Monrau, Elder Kent, Eddard, and a few other elders made the ascent to the top of the mountain. Visits to this holy site has become busy as not seen in a very long time, so they were drawn into the busy atmosphere of the path. There were people from every tribe; there were many they couldn't recognize. Before the goddess, all men were equal. No master, no servant. Though elves were seldom seen coming to worship, they were free to come and go as they please. Elves were not allowed to serve here.

Priests were selected from young men who apply to become one. Application was done by the aspirant making a pilgrimage to the shrine. The aspirant makes an offering and talks to one of the many priests in the temple. He is escorted to see the Master Recruiter who accepts his application and tells him to go home and return at an appointed time. It is at this time that his initiation process begins.

Women were excluded from this priesthood. The deity worshiped here is a goddess, of the beloved of the Lama, the god of light. It is said that all that is, was created by her. Sofeeya gave birth to all that existed. She decreed that only men would serve her as a form of revenge for Lama's offense against her. Lama had abandoned her to marry the moon goddess, she was beautiful and seduced Lama. Heartbroken, Sofeeya had descended to earth and made her home on this mountain. Women could come and worship and beg for favors and they were granted their requests but none was permitted to serve at her temple as priest.

The end of the path leads to a cave called the Sigil. Upon entering, the cave looked very large and well lighted with little Tallis lamps scattered all over the place. The walls had drawings of different colors depicting scenes from Creation. Each potion of the walls showed the creation of an element or thing in nature. Many people were drawn to a potion of the cave walls which depicted scenes for the creation of mankind. It showed how Lama made love to Sofeeya, the goddess of the Temple, and from this the first man and woman came. The wall was filled with scenes of lovemaking, making it a subject of admiration, especially among the younger pilgrims.

Monrau shook his head when a group of young men hurried past him to see the wall. Adjacent that wall, there is a path that leads to the highest point of the mountain. It was here that the statue of the goddess was worshiped. She kneels as she contemplates her creation and stares at the rising sun, who was once her lover and had left her for the moon goddess, Shimir. She doesn't look angry, neither does she look sad. She looks like she is in deep thought and contemplation. Monrau and the elders walked up that path and turned left, then right. They have come to see the Priest Kashi. He was one of the highest-ranking priests, they had in the counsel room, close to the goddess.

Monrau removed his headdress upon entering the Priest's room. The elders other did the same. They sat on stools. The priest knows why they have come, he had been informed ahead of the visit. He picked a scroll from one of the many holes that served as shelves in the room and opened slowly like one who had bitter news to tell.

The room was properly lit with Tallis lamps, the same as the ones in the other parts of the temple. Upon entering the room, the visitors were welcomed into a part that looked like a study. There were rolls of scrolls stacked in the holes in the wall. There was a large table; a large chair, where the priest sat and a wooden screen wall that separated this part of the room from the rest. The visitors would assume that the rest of the room were his living quarters. Only high ranking priests such as Kashi had rooms in the Sigil. The Archpriest lives alone in a secluded place, on the other side of the mountain. He is the head priest, but his name comes from him wearing an arc-shaped hat on his head.

"It is the new one who bears the scars". Kashi

begins. "The Old bears the load and thinks it mercy". Monrau responds. Kashi, my friend, you have never been hard to understand when we speak. Tell me in plain words what your heart bears to tell us. Kasha repeats, this time looking straight into Monrau's eyes with a look mixed with worry, fear, and surprise. It is the new one who bears the scars, the Old one bears the load and thinks its mercy. He continued. "The wise man is one who knows when to fight and when to retreat, such a man lives till the end of his days. There is a prophecy about the End of Days and it is already upon us. The sages speak of water turning into fire and land disappearing into the great abyss. The moon hasn't appeared for two moon cycles now and this has not happened for a thousand years. I suggest that you visit Sibylla. Only she will tell you what you need to do. As priests, it is our duty to watch as things happened and note them down. This scroll in my hand tells of the last purge and what the Nuhu, the great of the East did. You will need it and you will need men to burn as a holocaust to the pettiness of the gods'. Up till this time, everyone in the room has been silent. Kent spoke up. "Kashi, where shall we find Sibylla? The last time anyone saw her was in

Pisidia. She seems to have gone into oblivion".

"You can find her at Tarlamun, her mother's birth place, Kashi said. Ask from the market women when you get there, she is very popular with them". After some small talk, Monrau rose and all the men rose with him. He thanked Kashi profusely and handed him the gifts they had brought. One by one, they left the room. They went to pay homage to the goddess before they went back home.

Sibylla

To days later, Monrau, Kent, Lasama, and Eddard boarded a ship and left for Tarlamun. Wolzart was left as leader of the tribe in the absence of Monrau. It took five days to travel. The winds were favorable, they got there four days after they left.

The fishing town of Tarlamun was filled with people in every corner. The air was filled with birds, preying on carcasses of decaying fish. The smell of these decaying carcasses filled the air. The laughter of the returning fisherman, returning from their voyage, greeted Monrau and his men. Market women were there too. Some slim, some fat, most of them were in their middle years.

There was noise all around, as was usual with a marketplace. This did not seem to impress on Monrau who had a stony grin face of a warrior and the composed, reflective demeanor of a leader. In all his years, Kashi had never spoken to him in that manner, using proverbs and figurative speech. It dawned on him that he too did understand what was going on and can only hope that Sibylla had answers. Monrau was awakened from his thoughts when Eddard nudged him in the arm to tell him he knew where Sibylla lived. He had been told by one of the women. True to Kashi's word, she was popular among them.

The walk to Sibylla's house was not long. It took a few turns and asking. Her house was a moderate Victorian house with flowers lined around the front porch. An elf appeared at the door to welcome them. They told the elf where they had come from and the purpose of their visit. The elf, being used to people calling at the house at any time of day, went away to fetch his mistress. The house had a different color on every wall. Thought the colors matched. There were no paintings or any decorative artwork on any of the walls. The chairs were soft and comfortable, not something they would find in their tribe. They were used to hard furniture, rocky land, and harsh weather. It would seem that Sibylla has made a fortune for herself from the gift that has been given her by gods. The elf returned with cups of fresh milk and some baked loaves of bread. He set them on the table and informed them that his mistress would join them soon as she was on a visit to help a woman who had gone into labor.

Monrau fell into deep thoughts again. This time his bushy eyebrows arched, almost touching each other. The time the Zorostars had attacked his tribe, he was at war with the Druids as a mercenary soldier. He had to abandon the war and return home. The tribe had always faced one problem or another but in recent years, it was becoming worse; things didn't seem to get better. When he became chief a few years ago, an old woman had come to him at night. He was walking back from pouring liquid waste from his body when she met him in his tracks in the opposite direction. She had white and gray hair. Her face was joyful but her hands were bloody. She touched him on the chest and walked away. There was no bloodstain on his clothes, but he felt a hot sensation on his chest. He had told no one of that experience, he could not make any sense of what had happened to him and he didn't think anyone would. Two moons later, there was the cry of a Banshee heard in the woods behind his tent. Days later, news came that the witch of Calabrio had died.

There was noise in an inner room and some elves were seen running away from the room and into another room. They had their hands on their heads like they had been beaten on the head. An angry woman's voice was heard throwing commands. After a moment of quiet, Sibylla came into the room where the men were seated. She was a very young woman, not exactly pretty but whose looks would catch a man's attention. She had large piercing eyes and brown skin color like the Numidians. She apologized for keeping them, explaining the plight of the new mother who was near death during childbearing.

She told them, she knew why they had come and she would speak with them on the matter of their visit, when they came to her shrine. She clapped her hands quickly and two elves appeared. She gave instructions and went into the house.

Monrau was up and ready to meet the seer. The

other men stood up as well, ready. The elves led them through a doorway and into a room. The room was nothing like the room they had been in. It seemed like they had been taken into a cave, like the room of Kisha. The room was poorly lighted and smelt spices from Araba or some aromatic leaves. It had stone walls and engravings on them. The floor is like the floor of a cave. Nothing seemed like the room where they had been served milk and bread, it seemed they had left the house and were in some other place. Sibylla sat on a high chair. Her large piercing eyes were closed, her hair tied in a bun.

When they were seated, she opened her eyes and looked intensely at all of them, one by one. Sibylla spoke in a soft tone, "The Lion with its claws like iron and breath of fire has awakened. It will wrestle with the sun and eat it. That child of the Leviathan has come. Beware, the End of days is here". Monrau spoke first. "What can be done, what will avert this danger?" Sibylla was silent for a long time and said, "When the time has come, free the girl child in your keeping, let her marry whomever she liked and save us all from damnation". Everyone turned and looked at Monrau. Monrau, who was embarrassed and with askance on Sibylla. She smiled and told him to listen to her story about how it all began, it would all make sense to him.

Sibylla said "Cry not, O man, for vengeance will now be taken on the house of the diviners. Every last one of them will die". These were the exact words the Witch of Calabrio had told him that night, many years ago, as she touched his chest.

Sibylla's Story

In the beginning... "...There was chaos. Out of chaos was born darkness and light. The light was called Lama, darkness Amun. There was constant fighting, even from the womb of their mother Chaos, there was no love between them. They always fought over everything. One day, while they were fighting, Amun pushed Lama whose body hit their mother, who was returning from a visit to her father. She fell into a deep ditch in the center of the earth and died. Enraged, their grandfather sought to kill them both. They escaped to earth to be far away from grandfather Time. They were remorseful over the death of their mother and decided to live amicably".

"Sometime later, Lama fell in love with a young woman. She was modest, courteous though she was not pretty. She was the daughter of the god of seasons. She was known for her wisdom and deep insight into matters that were difficult to understand. She was always reserved and reflective. Lama made advances to her and she accepted and became his lover. She was so in love with Lama that she was willing to be his wife but Lama did not seem ready to marry her. Their frequent lovemaking created the stars, vegetation and every animal including men. The couple, though unmarried, were the envy of every god including Amun. They wished to have Sofeeya for their wife but she would not let them. Her wisdom made boundaries between the sea and land and helped her father rule over the seasons. Because of her wisdom and courtly manner, she convinced Lama and Amun to put aside their differences and share their rule over men. Twelve hours for the lama and the rest for Amun. Amun desires to have her by every means so he convinces Shimir to seduce Lama. Shimir goes into Lama's chamber one night when he was drunk and went into his bed. She seduces and sleeps with him, making him think she was Sofeeya. When it was time to go, for his twelve hours of rule, he discovered that it wasn't Sofeeya but Shimir in his bed. Sofeeya, having found out during the night, went to her father's house and refused to see Lama anymore. Shimir refuses to leave Lama, else she would tell the gods of his plans to seize power from the god of seasons".

"Shimir blackmails Lama into marrying her by offering to give Amun secrets on how to rule her younger brother Sun. According to Shimir's plan, Sun was his companion while she was to accompany Amun on his nightly rounds. Lama gives in to the arrangement. When she learned that Lama still yearned for Sofeeya by his side, she got angry and released the secrets to Amun. When Shita, the Sun god found out he was furious and his anger is felt when he gets to the peak of the day. This is his attempt to burn out the light".

"She created dark magic and gave those powers to some men who accepted her as a goddess. Her goal is to incite men against the light and in doing so cause him to lose popularity and his place among the gods. These worshipers of hers were the first diviners. They foretold of the day when Amun would share with them the secrets of the sun and they would get a spell to conquer and rule the son".

"Lama and Shimir never bore children".

Back to the present...

Monrau understood the meaning of the story. The diviners were at war with them, a war that had begun since the dawn of time. Killing the diviners will unleash more of their evil power into the universe and which will corrupt more people "Cry not, O man, for vengeance will be now, be taken on the house of the diviners. Every last one of them will die". Now those words seemed to make some sense to him. But how will they die? Who will carry out vengeance? Killing a diviner is no small feat, it was war! The Zorostars were that house and by his sword or by another every last one of them will die.

Monrau stood up to leave.

Dwarfs

The throne room of Kharis, the Dwarf King, was Spartan, as the lifestyle of the dwarves. Monrau had already been to that room several times to enter into commercial agreements, but this time it was different, what he was going to ask Kharis was a huge thing, it was something from which it was not possible to go back. Monrau had known Kharis for a long time, but he was not sure whether the Dwarf King wanted to follow them into the war.

Dwarves could be very loyal to allies. They were the kind of person who would take their clothes off for you, who would sacrifice their best soldiers to save you, but, at the same time, the Dwarves could be the worst allies in the world. That race could have been careless and cowardly. The story was full of episodes of betrayal by the dwarves for trivial reasons, and Monrau had always used

31

his diplomatic skills with Kharis. For now, everything had gone in the right direction, but everything could still change.

Kharis was seated on the throne, his thin face beginning to show signs of age. Kharis was a thousand years old, he was no longer a young dwarf, but he was not an old man either. Monrau was sure that there was still the energy for battles inside him, but the problem was to get her out.

Kharis' eyes were fixed on Monrau, the Dwarf King wanted to hear the man's words, and only then would he make his decision.

"Monrau, son of Biggis, you had not honored me with your visit for a long time".

"King Kharis, son of Karloff, is an honor to be here before you. I am your humble servant, command, and I will obey".

"You said you had to send me a very important message. Let's not waste any more time, tell me everything, I'll listen to you".

"Our village has been under attack for some time. We are sure it is the work of a Nandi Bear".

"It's been years, decades, that monster didn't attack. Why did it happen?"

"You know".

"The prophecy?"

"The time is now, now is the time to act. We can't stand still and get killed. Today it's the men, tomorrow it's the dwarves. The Diviners want to dominate everything".

"What do you want from me, Monrau, son of Biggis?"

"We men want to declare war on the Diviners. Our ancestors have defeated them, and we can do it again".

"Do you believe those old legends?"

"The legends are true stories. But we cannot fight alone, we need allies, as in the Legendary War. Altogether we have already defeated the Diviners, and they have waited until now for their revenge. We have forgotten the story, and we didn't watch them properly. But the blood of the brave warriors who won the Legendary War flows through us, and I feel it burning in my veins! "

"These are beautiful words, Monrau, son of Biggins. But what do you want from my people and me?"

"We men and you dwarves have been allies for centuries. We want to declare war on the Diviners once and for all. We need your help, in memory of our alliance, and the sacrifice of the thousand human warriors in the siege of Holla. You can't have forgotten it, you were there with them, and if you are alive, it is only thanks to the death of my ancestors".

"I know you don't have to remind me".

"We can't win alone, but united we stand, divided we fall".

King Kharis thought silently.

"No".

"What?"

"I can't go to war with you".

"Why did you become a coward?"

"I am not a coward. I have seen a thousand wars

before your birth, and I will see many after your death. I do not fear death in battle, and I want an honorable death that will be remembered forever. But I am not stupid, and my first duty is the good of my people, not my personal glory".

"You also know that the Diviners will also arrive here, it is a matter of time. The Nandi Bear can dig into the ground and reach you at any time. Now is the time to attack".

"Monrau, you are young, and you have never seen a war. I can understand you, even I was like that during my youth. My blood was burning with desire, I wanted to live a battle and win. I felt immortal. But I saw soldiers killed in horrible ways and madness in the eyes of the survivors. When I became King, I swore that I would think about the good of my people and that I would declare war only if necessary. The Diviners never offended us, I don't want to be the first to attack them".

"You are making a serious mistake, King Kharis, and you are violating our alliance".

"You know my word is sacred. The dwarves would

die rather than betray a covenant written in blood, but the good of my people is superior. If I were a normal dwarf, I would be on the front line with you, but I can't do it; I have responsibilities".

"Is there anything that can change your mind?"

"If and when we are attacked, the situation will change. I want to be honest with you, Monrau, son of Biggis. My people are unable to stand a war. Our days of proud warriors are long gone. Young people have grown up in peacetime, old warriors no longer have the energy to make a difference in battle. If we go to war, we will die, and I don't want to be remembered as the King who annihilated his people".

"I understand. I'll have to look for other allies".

"I know well that you are already looking for them, Monrau, son of Biggis. And I know that you will report my refusal to him. This conversation is over, I will not change my mind, and you would risk compromising our relationships. You need allies now, not enemies. If you start the war, you will have enemies in abundance, it makes no sense to add new ones".

"I understand. I am sincere with you, King Kharis, I did not expect these words".

"Don't make your position worse with me. My patience has a limit. I just want to know one thing: who have you identified as other allies?"

"The Valkyries and the Elves. Perhaps the Kobolds".

"I want to give you some advice, also in memory of the friendship that bound me to your father. Concentrate on humans, strengthen your charisma on them, and make sure they don't run away at the first difficulty. The war you want to win is hard, many people believe , and you will be close to them, and you will see them suffer in indescribable ways. This could break you or make you stronger. I don't know, and maybe you don't know either. Strengthen your ascendancy over men, follow my advice, or this war will be lost even before fighting the first battle".

"Thanks for your advice".

King Kharis got off the throne and went near

Monrau. The dwarf touched him and smiled.

"Let's not be grudging, Monrau, son of Biggis. I want to see you here as a winner".

"I hope so. And I hope with all my heart that you have not made the wrong choice".

"I'm not perfect, and only time will tell. You can go".

Monrau left the very depressed throne room. He had thought he could get help from the dwarves in the impending war, but he hadn't been able to convince Kharis. Monrau was not stupid, he understood the responsibilities that a King had, but he could not fail to be disappointed.

Was it proof that he wasn't a real leader? Or could nobody convince Kharis?

Eddard and the other Elders were traveling to get other tribes to join the fight. Their mission was easier, everyone had lost a brother, sister, children, or friends in the forests, and everyone hated the Nandi Bears. That was an opportunity to take revenge. Diviners could die like them, their magic and monsters could not save them forever. Everyone knew it, but going to war was different.

Monrau hoped for the success of Eddard and the others, it was necessary to have allies.

The man came out of the bowels of the Sacred Mountain of the dwarves, and saw the blue sky, without a cloud, and the forest in the distance. From that distance, it all seemed harmless, and Monrau felt a sense of peace, something she hadn't felt for some time.

Then he thought about all the people killed. He had to avenge them; it was his duty, and then to live his life to the fullest. It was the duty of those who survived, and he would do it.

He had to go talk to the Queen of the Valkyries, it was essential to convince them to join the fight.

Queen of Valkyries

R elations between men and Valkyries had never been simple. The Valkyries adored the war, and for them, every opportunity was perfect to jump into the fray of the battle without thinking about the consequences. Men did not always have their desire to launch into the next war, and for this reason, the Valkyries often considered men weak, and not worthy of respect.

Respect was fundamental for the Valkyries, who believed that a person who did not deserve to be respected did not even deserve to live. The history of man was full of attacks by Valkyries on villages commanded by leaders they did not respect and of brutal massacres. The Valkyries did not do it for evil purposes, but only for the thrill of the battle and to eliminate people from the world who did not deserve respect. If you wanted to impress a Valkyrie, you had to try to get her respect, one way or

41

another, and that was what Monrau's father had done.

Biggis had been a great warrior, one of the few to defeat the Queen of Valkyries in a duel, and who, for this gesture, had gained an ally for eternity.

But now Biggis was dead, and it was Monrau who had to earn the Queen's respect. It was not enough to invite them to war. The Valkyries also knew that the Visors were very powerful enemies, and had not yet attacked them.

This does not mean that they were afraid of it, but those warriors understood when it was time to attack and when to defend and wait, and that was the moment of defense.

At least until Monrau's proposal.

And the man really hoped for it.

What would have happened if the Valkyries refused? The only hope would have been the elves, great soldiers, but not enough to win. Monrau had to convince at least two races to join them or die in the attempt. The man would not have endured the humiliation of going home without having even reached an agreement.

Monrau's bad mood was worsened by the presence of a white bird flying around him. Was it a Caladrius, the bird that appeared, to who was going to die?

Monrau didn't want to think about that superstition, but he was stronger than him.

He was afraid, and the Valkyries would notice it.

He had to mask it, or the mission of finding allies would have been impossible.

The hall of Asya, the Queen of the Valkyrie, was decorated with weapons and war paintings. The Queen wore an elegant leather bodice and short pants that showed off her legs. He had leather shoes on his feet, and around his waist was a belt with a diamond-studded dagger. It was the legendary dagger of Asya, a lethal weapon, which the Queen knew how to throw in a single second. Nobody had managed to survive that dagger.

The woman looked at Monrau with ill-concealed contempt.

"Man, speak, but my time is precious. Tell me immediately what you want".

"I am Monrau, son of Biggis".

"I know your father, his death has saddened me. A great warrior. Tell me what you want".

"Your majesty, I come on behalf of all my people to ask for your alliance for the war we want to declare to the Visors".

"Why do you want to declare war on the Visors?"

"Our races have always been enemies, and my ancestors defeated them in battle. The Visors have never forgotten what happened, and they want revenge. And I believe those people just want to create chaos in the world. They unleashed the Nandi Bears against us, and we've had too many mourners. We can't wait any longer, it's time to fight back".

"I respect those who want to fight back, but I do not respect those who died. If they are dead, it is because they are weak. Don't talk further, I know you want my alliance for your war, don't you?"

"Exactly, my Queen. Without the Valkyries, we won't win".

"Why do we have to help you? For what reason?"

"I know that the Visors are also enemies of the Valkyries. You will be the next target. And I know well that a glorious battle is what every Valkyrie dreams of. There will never be a war like this again, and the history books will tell the warriors' exploits winners forever".

"You're right, the Visors are our enemies, and a Valkyrie never refuses a battle. But we never fight with those we don't respect. Give me a reason to respect you".

"Your Majesty."...

"Don't talk, we don't respect words, we respect actions. War is pain, fear, and suffering. Are you afraid of suffering?"

"No".

"We will see. Are you willing to do anything to earn my respect?"

"Yes".

"I said anything. Did you understand correctly?"

"My hearing is perfect, and I understand exactly".

"Very well. Then you will now try to earn my respect".

Asya rose from her throne while her maidservants surrounded Monrau. The man could not escape, nor could he fight against all those expert warriors.

"Undress him, the time has come for the test of blood and courage," said Asya.

The maids immobilized Monrau and stripped him, leaving only the undergarments. The man was stuck in his arms and legs, and the hold of the Valkyries was indestructible. Those women stopped the charge of the Nandi Bears with their hands, holding Monrau was child's play.

"Now, we will check if you are really willing to do anything to get my respect. I will test your body, your mind, and your will. It will not be pleasant. You can give up when you want, but you will lose my respect". Asya said, approaching with a stick in her hand.

"This is no ordinary wood, it is wood of the Millar tree, which has a thousand poisonous quills. You will have hallucinations, and all your most hidden fears will appear. No man can bear the sight of this horror for a long time. Your father has endured for ten strokes and touched the madness. I want to see what you can do".

Monrau didn't even have time to respond, because Asya moved quickly and hit him in the back with the stick. The pain was terrible, Monrau had the feeling of being hit by a thousand needles at the same time. Monrau felt the blood flow on his back, and panic began to seize him.

Second hit. The pain increased, the man sweated.

Images began to appear in his mind. They were fantasy, but they were so real that Monrau was afraid. The Visors had won the war, the heads of Eddard and the other Elders were on spades, and Monrau was the only one still alive.

The man was in chains, defeated, and humiliated. History would have remembered him as the leader who had destroyed his people.

Third hit.

The Visors discussed his fate. Killing it? Too easy. Monrau had to suffer from what he had done. Suffer for a long time.

Fourth hit.

Fifth hit.

Sixth hit.

Monrau didn't want to give up, but horror was happening in his mind.

Torture scenes so realistic as to make Monrau scream. A Nandi Bear who ate his heart and magic of the Visors that immediately made him regenerate.

A Visor who used him as a guinea pig for a series of experiments.

Seventh hit.

Eighth hit.

Monrau had reached the limit of endurance. Those images were so real ... unbearable. The torturer poured molten gold into his throat, and a Visor brought him back to life to once again inflict that torture on him. Eat the putrid meat of the other Elders.

That was the fate of the defeated; it was what Monrau deserved.

Ninth hit.

Tenth hit.

Monrau screamed in pain and passed out. His back reduced to a heap of blood and flesh. Asya looked at him and threw the stick away.

"You have earned my respect, Monrau. But it is useless, you are dead. You had to accept your limitations, a corpse is not needed for this war".

The Queen of the Valkyries returned to sit on her throne and ordered them to prepare for war.

"Monrau's sacrifice must not be forgotten. We will win the war and defeat the Visors. We will enter the history books". the Queen said to her maidservants, ordering him to gather generals and soldiers. They had to plan the correct strategy to attack and win because a Valkyrie only fights to win.

Then Asya looked at Monrau's body.

"Clean up the body, and bring it back to his tribe. I want this man to be buried with all honors. He got my respect by paying with his life.

One of Asya's maidservants approached the body, then let out a scream of fright. Monrau was a knee, full of blood, but with a determined look.

"One more ."... he said in a weak voice.

Asya came over to hear better. The Queen didn't believe her ears, and she couldn't understand what was going on. Was that man alive? No one but Biggis had ever endured ten hits, and did that man ask for another one?

"What did you say?" asked the Queen.

"One more ... the test is not over. I have not abandoned it".

"You already have my respect, I will go to war with you, it is not necessary".

"One more ... I have to end my nightmare".

"You may not survive, it's a miracle that you've survived until now".

"I have to do it. You don't know what I saw".

"As you wish".

Eleventh hit.

Monrau collapsed back to the ground in pain. This blow is very strong, stronger than all the others. The vision is short but chilling.

Monrau's head on a pike, but alive. Ants walking on the face and birds that eat the eyes. Eternal suffering while the body is thrown into the fire.

That was fate in the event of defeat, and there was no escape. The war was beginning, and Monrau could no longer avoid the war.

Win, or this will be your destiny.

The man's body was shaken by strong convulsions and then vomited a strange black liquid. After vomiting, the pain disappeared immediately.

"You threw up the poison of the stick. Now you

have to rest. My doctors will medicate your back so as not to risk infections. You have my word that we will fight for you. I don't want to know what you saw, but I know it was horrible. The Valkyries are with you, Monrau, son of Biggis".

Monrau was happy, then passed out, falling into a dreamless sleep.

A Messenger of Evil

The Hall of Gathering was full of people, and Queen Asya's presence stood out among all men. The Queen of the Valkyries had wanted to go to the first war council in person to observe her allies and carefully plan the strategy. The Queen despised many of the men present, except Monrau and a few other warriors, but she had given her word on her loyalty, and a queen always respects the commitments she has made.

Several men observed the beautiful Valkyrie, it was the first time that many of them observed that legendary creature, and it could be the last.

Monrau took the floor for the opening speech. The man had recovered from the beating suffered by the Queen of the Valkyries, his mind was more intelligent than ever, but the back would always have been furrowed by scars. Monrau was proud to have those marks on his skin, they were proof of his courage.

"Friends, brothers, sons of my own mother, my heart is full of pride in seeing you here. It means that you believed in my words, in the words of Elder Eddard and of all the other valiant warriors you see here with us. You shared our anger towards the Visors, and you believe that the time has finally come to do justice, once and for all. The only allies that are missing are the Elves because Kind Daniz did not want to receive me. I am disappointed by their behavior, and I want to try to talk to them again shortly, but for the moment, I want to say that the people I see before my eyes make me understand that we have already won this war! "

Everyone cheered, hearing those words. Monrau had been able to mask the disappointment of King Daniz's attitude. The Elven King had even refused to receive him, saying he had no time and interest in sacrificing resources in a war that primarily involved humans.

The Elves were creatures who did not like war, but had always been excellent allies of men, especially from a commercial point of view. Was a war bad for business?

Yes, of course, but it was not enough reason not to talk to Monrau. The man would have been able to handle a refusal of the alliance, as had happened with the dwarves, but King Kharis had had the decency to say it in person. King Daniz had left Monrau outside the castle doors to find an explanation for the behavior.

Were the Elves allied with the Visors? No, impossible, the fire was more likely to freeze, or a cowardly Valkyrie was born. The Elves despised everything of the Visors, and would have preferred to die rather than join them, Monrau was sure of that.

"The Visors humiliated us, made us feel fear, terror, the feeling of not being able to defend ourselves. We suffered for our mourning, we lost talented and courageous young people, who did not deserve to die like that. The Visors hit us to the heart, but they did not get their result. We are still standing, stronger than before, and the time for revenge has arrived! We will win the war, we will wipe out the Visors, and we will begin a new era! "

Everyone was screaming with joy.

A scream rose.

"WAR! WAR! WAR! WAR!"

All the assembled people let out their war cry, which lasted for several minutes. Monrau had the feeling that at that moment, they were absolutely invincible, ready to exterminate every enemy.

"I want to thank the Valkyries for helping us in this battle. They are brave warriors who do not know fear and who know how to win every battle. Their help is invaluable, and the least we can do is try to fight with the utmost courage in every situation. The Valkyries will be our example in battle, and I want to thank Asya, the Queen of the Valkyries, for being with us today. Our people have a massive debt to your people, a debt that we will pay back sooner or later. my word".

"I don't need your word, Monrau, son of Biggis. Your honor is enough for me. We are friends in difficult times, and we will be friends even in peacetime, from now and as long as you are alive".

The blood of the Valkyries never failed. Asya

respected Monrau, and it was up to the other warriors to get her respect. If they had made it, the Valkyries would have been allies forever.

"I would also like to thank all the tribes who have accepted our request for help and have shown themselves to be altruistic in moments of selfishness. You are the reason I fight because I know that every soldier, every ally, friend, and brother, is ready to give their life for me, and I'm ready to do the same! The Visors are powerful, but they are selfish and vain, every wizard fights for himself and for his glory, even if they never admit it. We are united and fight for our ideal, for our future, and we know we can trust each other. This is our strength! We are a chain, and they cannot break us! "

Other screams of joy. Monrau was drunk with that feeling of power, he was his first time as a leader, and it was a wonderful feeling, better than sex. At that moment, Monrau could defeat anyone and was not afraid of anything or anyone.

The warriors continued to speak, planning attacks and strategies. There was no need to declare war because it started at the time of the first Nandi Bears attack. The Visors knew that they would attack, sooner or later.

The best strategy was a quick and immediate attack. The land of the Visors was far away, but they could reach it in three days, riding quickly. The wizards were locked in their castle, where they studied new spells and evil arts, their strength was not the art of war, but the use of magic and the evocation of monsters. They had to defeat them and then kill all the wizards to win the war, and it wouldn't have been easy. The Visors were not stupid enough to get them to the castle without any trap, and they had to provide constant supplies and medical care to the whole army.

Monrau was impatient to leave, but everyone knew that it would not be possible to do it immediately. It took time, and to make sure that you were on the best, safest, and fastest path.

Elder Kent was the strategist, and he was working out the best path.

In the middle of the meeting, a soldier entered the hall, and announced the presence of an ambassador from

King Daniz, with a message of the utmost importance.

Monrau gave orders to let him in, and a tall, platinum-haired elf entered the room. The elf was dressed in a splendid uniform with gold finishes and with the coats of arms of ancient noble families. Monrau did not know him, but it was evident that he was the son of some nobleman or one of the attendants of King Daniz.

Had the King changed his mind?

"Sorry for the delay and the way I got there. My name is Kobbs, and I represent his majesty, the immortal King Daniz. I have the honor of bringing his words to your ears. The Immortal King apologizes for his behavior towards Monrau, son of Biggis. It was not the King's intention to offend him. In any case, the King intends to clarify his position personally with Monrau and his honorable allies, and tomorrow he will go here to speak privately. The King hardly leaves his castle, and this is a great honor for you. Accept it with the respect that is due to the Immortal King".

Kobbs stopped talking.

"We are honored to receive King Daniz. I have so many things to ask him," said Monrau".Thanks for letting us know".

"I warned you, but you will have died before his arrival!" Kobbs yelled, drawing a small dagger and throwing himself on Monrau, who had been petrified by what was happening.

Elder Kent got in the way and was stabbed in the chest, collapsing on the ground. Asya had already thrown herself on Kobbs and hit him in the heart with her dagger.

Kobbs fell to the ground without a whimper, and a strange black cloud came out of his mouth.

The cloud took on a vaguely human form.

"You were lucky, Monrau. You will die next time". said a loud and evil voice, which filled the whole hall with his presence.

"Who are you"?

"I'm nobody, but my owner is Aldair of the Visors. This is just a taste of what we can do if you really go to war against us. Daniz and the elves are already under the mental control of Mantis of the Visors, and you will be wiped out before you even get to the high castle. You can surrender now and become our slaves, or face your destiny. The choice is yours".

Asya roared with anger and hurled her dagger at the cloud. The weapon went through it and crashed into the wall.

"You are braver than intelligent, Valkyrie. We have some unfinished businesses with you, and this war will allow us to eliminate you forever, something that we should have been doing for a long time".

"We are not afraid of you," said Asya.

"We will wipe you out, once and for all," said Monrau.

"Aren't you afraid? Oh, I promise you that you will have a lot of them". said the voice, laughing.

Suddenly a strong earthquake shook the hall, and the cloud of smoke disappeared into thin air. All the warriors looked around, not entirely understanding what was happening. The Visors' message was crystal clear, and the army was also supposed to fight against the Elves, it was the worst possible scenario.

"Do you still want to fight"? Asya asked.

"Now more than ever," said Monrau.

The Fever of Blood

There was the feel of war everywhere. It had dyed most people with excitement. Fighters on Monrau's side ran across streets chanting rhythmic songs that made chicken-hearted kids cower into their shells. Those who could endure thunderous thudding feet stood a step away from their doors and chanted the songs with their fear still keeping them at alert.

People filled their homes with food and other items that the war could have prevented them from getting. The diviners were not easy tissue to chew, but Monrau, the son of Biggies, would never give in so easily. With the Valkyries forming an ally with them now, they believed that this was the time to humble the diviners.

Monrau himself trained with the people from the moment the sun was an infant hanging in the sky until it aged and the moon took over. After a busy day, Monrau

63

would gather some children around him to tell them stories that he considered interesting. But tonight was different. Monrau walked like his ankles were shackled and he felt his head palpitate with ache. An uncanny bitter taste hung on his tongue and he wouldn't say a word to the children who were gathered around him and waiting for him to tell them stories of wars and gone glories. He hissed, shook his head and stared at the sky as he lay belly-up in front of his hut.

That night, the children walked away from one after the other. Their sluggish steps missed the excitement in hopping back home after hearing those stories. They all knew that Monrau was ill and could even die before the war started. The second day, parents of those children came to greet Monrau, each with a strand of palm leaf which symbolized wishes for peace and good health. They were surprised that he could not even say a word to reply to their greetings. He only nodded and gesticulated. Despite his ill state, he never lost his smile. He managed to smile and nod at each visitor that greeted him and wished him quick recuperation. He smiled despite the weakness. He wished that the news had not spread this much because people would obviously be thrown into panic. He wished he could speak to recuperate quickly.

When the parents left, many of Monrau's soldiers came around. They were weighed down heavily with sorrows. For about three days, Monrau couldn't leave his recliner, but to lift the spirits of the soldiers, he lifted himself and sat upon the recliner. His face was oily and his eyes glistened as if they would shed tears soon, but he was smiling instead. They spoke words of encouragement and wished him quick recuperation before leaving one after the other. But one of the soldiers waited behind, he is Averyi. Averyi was the laziest soldier he knew in his troop. Monrau had wiped him a hundred times. He had made the boy uproot woods where he had found him sleeping at the foot of the tree. It was the night he decided to expel him that the sickness started yet he sat, the boy raining tears for his master's condition.

"I will have to journey back home and tell my father about your state of health…he will surely know what to do about it".

Monrau was quiet.

"Or shall we just go to Valkyrie? Asya could be of help", the boy moved closer and said. "She offered to always help, she will help us this time, we can't win the war without you. Everybody is down already". When Averyi realized that Monrau couldn't say a word, he hugged him and promised that he would be fine. He was outside when he met Asya on the way. She had heard of Monrau's sudden illness and come to greet him and proffer whatever solution she had in mind.

The subsequent morning, Averyi journeyed from the city center and crossed rivers and hills back to their hamlet where his father lived. He was the healer of the community and could heal any form of ailments. Averyi told him about his master's state of health and the possibility of war. He offered that they should journey back to the city to rescue Monrau before he died of the illness, but even Averyi's father was afraid that he would lose him. He knew how weak his son could be. He didn't even know that he could journey so far on foot.

They rested for a day and started going the day after. When they got there, they met Monrua, still bedridden. He could not even smile, the only sign of life was breathing. Averyi's father gave him four gourds containing some drugs that could be helpful. He examined Monrau's eyes and mouth and shook his head. Averyi and other people around knew that there was something amiss already. They had less than a week before the war started, yet here was one of the leading fighters in bed.

"No one on earth, or in air, or on the water can cure this illness. We would have been considering dumping him in some water if not for the existence of Caladrius".

"Caladrius… that's the snow-white bird".

"Good boy", the father was so proud of him. He never knew that Averyi could mark all that he had said and describe the bird bears as angels of the sky…

"Let me tell you a little tale about the bird", Averyi's father said. "This bird doesn't look at someone who is sick. The bird could heal a sick individual after it had taken all the illnesses on anyone. Once the bird takes the illness on itself, it spreads it to space so it could disappear. In the process, he would cure himself of the illness too".

But they had to find it first before they could talk about any other thing.

"Father, where can we find this bird? I'm ready to go look for it even if it resides at the south of the earth".

"I'd grant your wish to go, but not without a few other soldiers. It could be very dangerous there".

"Yes, father. But it would be good if we can just get the bird as early as possible. The war starts soon and the enemies never rest".

"Now the bird would have left Valkyeries, we would have told the Valkyrie queen to bring it here. But as the gods have shown it, it is journeying towards the realm of the elves".

"Even if it goes to the belly of hell, I will go bring it", Averyi stood up and stamped his foot on the earth as he spoke.

Surprised, his father stared at him and said, "this man has really made you a man like him. You're a warrior. Go summon five other soldiers with you and leave for the city of the elves. I will give you this", he offered Averyi a small hollow bamboo. "Look through the hole with an eye and you'll see the bird anywhere it flies. It will enrich you with instincts that will make you feel the presence of danger or otherwise. It's a tool to lead the troop".

"Thank you, Father. Averyi collected the small bamboo, dipped it in his pocket and sped out of the dank room. He ran through the paths across the city, ignoring bewildered faces and voices that screamed his name. When he got to the barracks, he met soldiers at the front. Since they knew him, they let him in. He met the platoon leader asking him to give him five soldiers so they could go look for the bird.

"The bird is the only cure to Monrau's illness", he told the leader who instructed that the beagle be blown. As the sound ran through the barracks, members of the platoon were gathered in front of a hut where the leader used to see his people. The leader was a hefty man with a mustache that seemed to curve upwards. His voice was deep and firm just as his furrowed face.

"I have summoned you all here to tell you that a new war is coming up. Not the one with the elves and the Visors. It's with death this time".

"Death?" some of the soldiers chorused at once.

"Yes, death", the leader cleared his throat. "Death is about to claim Monrau, the national commander of our army, and we want five soldiers that are willing to die for him. This is the only way he can live. Remember that if we lose him, we're losing the war, and if we lose this war, you're likely losing your life as well".

"I'm going", a sinewy soldier stepped out with his thin arms glued to his sides.

"I am willing to die", another soldier stepped out. He was built and hairy.

About eight other soldiers stepped out after the two, confessing their willingness to die for Monrua. The platoon leader selected five out of the soldiers and told them to follow Averyi who would tell them everything they needed to know about the mission.

"This mission is going to make each of you forever a hero. It's a privilege and you must regard it as such. As you can see, many stepped out to help but only very few of you were chosen. So move on with the courage to win and we shall win!"

"We shall win! We shall win! We Shall Win" the soldiers chorused as they marched on towards the entrance to the barracks.

When they were about to reach the gate, Averyi quieted the soldiers and told them that they were not going to die.

"The mission here is to look for the caladrius bird. It would cure the illness".

"That's a very simple task then", the sinewy soldier said.

"Simple", other soldiers chorused and nodded.

"Now who leads the team? This will be given to the leader as a compass. Who will lead us?" Averyi asked. There was grave silence as one soldier looked at the other to volunteer to lead.

"Kalad should lead us", the bulky soldier said, looking at the tall, sinewy soldier. The other soldiers agreed and Avcryi gave me the hollow bamboo stick. He gave Kalad all the instructions and guided him on the functions of the stick before the journey to the country of the elves started. They journeyed quietly through the paths that led them into the Silent Forest which was known for its cemetery silence. The trees had a lot of fruit on them and they were very tasty and cold. Kalad made the troop sit for a while to eat some fruit and drink from a silently flowing river before they continued the journey. When they crossed a roaring river and to a forest where they heard a lot of birds singing, they knew that they had left Silent Forest but knew not the name of the new place. Seeing that many of them would have grown weak, Kalad decided to make everyone rest for a while.

They formed a circle sitting while Kalad stood and watched everywhere. When everyone but Averyi and Kalad was asleep, Averyi offered to watch over the soldiers but Kalad declined and ordered him to go and sleep. Averyi sulked at the command but turned to sleep near the rest of the soldiers. Hardly had he touched down when Kalad screamed for help. It was dark already and difficult to see what was really happening, but they could hear the flapping of wings. Before Sanzill, the bulky soldier could make a torch, a thud came from where Kalad stood. When the torch burnt, it revealed Kalad lying down with a dead white bird over his face. The bird plucked out his eyes, ate away his nose and he had also injured the bird in the neck.

The soldiers wept and dumped Kalad's remains inside the raging river where their salty tears mixed with the hasty water. The water splashed with joy as it took him in. It first savored the taste as it seemed to roll at a spot before it pushed the remains away from the sight of the colleagues. After he was gone, they moved back to their base and Averyi suggested that they chose another leader. This time, Sanzill, the bulky soldier was elected to lead. They didn't very much believe in Averyi, not only because he was skinny, but was also weak. They couldn't even hide their surprise that he was a member of the squad looking for the bird. Averyi himself would have taken advantage of having the stick in hand since his father had told him to lead them, but he still wouldn't impose himself on them. Besides, he also found it quite unimaginable to be the leader of the grown and built soldiers with much experience and skill all because they were looking for a bed.

After they had all mourned Kalad, the fallen leader, they decided to leave the spot and journeyed on. Sanzill peeked through the hollow in the bamboo. He didn't see any sign or have any feeling where the bird could be. They just moved on. They climbed a hill covered with green and sat there. The sun had subsided, yet the rock was hot, so some people stood and climbed a tree on the mountain. It had its roots holding on a very huge rock that had broken away from the mountain. Others stood and roamed the mountain staring down as if they would see the bird flying.

"The war is imminent. Averyi, sincerely, I'm afraid that this way will start before we are able to find this bird", Sanzill said. He was standing beside Averyi and looking at him right in the eyes. "Averyi, I'm really afraid".

"You don't have to be", Averyi managed to say. He had never imagined that Sanzill could be afraid of anything or even confused. He was always courageous. He always gave the best advice. He knew Sanzill might want to abdicate the position to someone at this juncture, but he was not even ready for such. He would rather watch and learn how and what a leader does than lead. He would rather choose to support.

"But I am, and I'm even surprised that I'm afraid. This is unlike me".

"Are we sleeping here?" Averyi asked, to swerve the topic away from fears.

"Although it appears safe, I would suggest we sleep at the foot of the mountain instead of the peak. It can be too cold at night".

"Yes, it's true. Direct exposure can cause an extreme cold".

"Averyi, I feel like… like you should just be the

one leading us".

"I?" his eyes ran around. What he had been trying to avoid was chasing him around already. "But I can't".

"You can, and you will. Summon the rest of us".

Averyi summoned other members of the troop and they all rushed to him, forming a circle around him and listening in absolute silence as he spoke and the wind whistled.

"I am grateful to you all for your loyalty so far. First of all, we must go down this mountain to avoid suffering from extreme cold and find a safe place to pass the night. Also, I would like to inform you that after I have led this team for almost a day, I feel like this role isn't actually mine. I understand that this might seem difficult to be acceptable to you, but the pure truth is that I don't feel like I can continue with this".

"Is this meant to be one of your expensive jokes?" Zill, the tallest and lightest of them said and chuckled.

"He is actually joking", Averyi laughed. He wanted others to reject Sanzill's offer to abdicate the position to him. "Sanzill you're physically and mentally fit to lead us. I am not seeing anyone taking this position yet".

"Yes, of course, no one else can do it but you", other members of the troop chorused and Sanzill wanted to cry.

"Averyi can do it", Sanzill said and others laughed. "I mean he is meant to do this task, you don't feel what I'm feeling now".

"We can't feel anything. Just lead us". Other members of the troop said and guffawed.

"Okay, let us leave this mountain first". Sanzill led them down the steep with his head buried. He held back tears as others joked about his attempt to abdicate the position. When they got down, Sanzill ordered that they made a makeshift tent where they would pass the night. They buried four about two feet of a six-feet tall wood with heads that formed Y and put some woods across them. Then they covered the woods with palm fronds.

That night, they slept under the shed on woven palm fronds. Although quite uncomfortable, they found the sleep quite satisfactory. Sanzill and Averyi woke up in the middle of the night to watch over the rest of the team members.

"Why not believe in yourself?" Sanzill asked.

"I wanted to ask you the same question". Averyi said as he sat on a makeshift bench and tickled the earth with a stick.

"You have the leadership potential in you. You may not see it yet, but I have seen your ability to convince others even against what they wanted".

"Is that all you need to be a leader?"

"That's not all but it carries a massive share in it", Sanzill cleared his throat and said. "And you're the only one standing by me when I'm troubled and even at this moment".

"That's the reason I can't lead. I would make a good follower", he coughed and dropped the stick in his hand. "Besides, who would even believe in me? I'm so young".

"Everyone will do so when you're ready for the

position. It's yours, as I feel it. Did you get what I'm trying to say?" Sanzill asked, but got no answer. The next thing, he heard Averyi snoring. "He must be tired already".

The subsequent morning, they dismantled the shed. Each person carried an item or two that made up the tent and they continued journeying. They walked until their legs ached from extreme trekking but Sanzill wanted them to continue the journey still.

"The bamboo compass wants us to walk a little bit further. It says there is a valley ahead of us where the bird resides", Sanzill said as he equally trudged behind the rest. He hadn't had a proper sleep since he had become the leader of the troop. Now he could barely keep the same pace with them, his head banged and his joins ached too. But he wouldn't tell anyone this. When they got to a steep that led a valley they called The Gape. They trod cautiously down the steep. Everywhere felt cool and scary because it was cold and quiet except for the bubbling of a stream below and various chirps of birds.

When they got to the river, they decided to have

their bath. Everybody stripped to bathe but Sanzill lay near the water and slept off. After the rest were done bathing, Averyi woke Sanzill up for a bath. Zill found some yams and decided to uproot them to roast.

While the yam roast and its smell claimed the atmosphere, Sanzill sat on the rock near the water and took his bath slowly and therapeutically. He washed out the dirt in his toenails and scrubbed every part that could save dirt diligently. When he was done bathing he stood up, turned and took his pants which was not too far away from him. He was still by the riverside and had a leg inside one of the hoses when he heard a splash and before he could look back a giant crocodile seized one of the legs and swiftly pulled him to the water which had turned red already. Sanzill turned and hit the crocodile's head with the bamboo compass in hand as he screamed, while other members of the troop attacked the crocodile with the shed woods and killed it. But one leg was already gone. Averyi and Zill helped Sanzill out of the water. He wept like a baby; the pain sent fire through his veins to the head as his colleagues tended the wound.

"Let's apply the sap of banana fronds. It can help stop the bleeding". Averyi said and Zill went with another member of the troop to tear the fronds of bananas.

They came back with a load of banana fronds and rubbed the broken part on the wound so it could absorb the sap. Sanzill screamed. Averyi checked his pocket and found a small gourd. He let some brownish powder on his palm mixed it with little water quantity until it became viscous and let Sanzill drink some. The bleeding stopped but Sanzill slept almost immediately. Others slept too, including Averyi. The body of the crocodile lay near them as if sleeping.

When Averyi woke up, he went straight to Sanzill who was still sleeping he patted him at the shoulder and he woke up.

"Looks like you're feeling better now". Averyi said.

"Yes, much better", Sanzill croaked. He managed to sit up looking at the leg and shaking his head. "I'm hungry".

"What are we doing about this crocodile? We dump

it into the water?"

"No, I want it eaten", Sanzill said and smiled. "I want to have a taste of it too".

"It ate your leg. That means we will be eating your leg too".

"As far as I'm concerned, what we eat is not my leg, it's an animal".

Averyi chuckled. By this time, other members of the troop had already woken up. Averyi told Zill to prepare the meat with other members of the troop.

"Averyi", Sanzill called as other members of the troop surrounded the meat and sang songs. "I want you to take the mantle of this leadership from me. I am ill and almost dying now. But can you do me this favor and take what belongs to you from me?"

"It doesn't belong to me. We can as well give it to another experienced person. Zill is there, Zao can do it. Give it to Mao, his elder brother".

"We haven't found this bird because you have delayed too much from taking responsibilities that are yours. You can as well give it to each of us until you're the only one left".

"Sanzill, what do you want me to do?"

"Summon the troop".

Averyi summoned other members of the troop and who gathered around quickly, abandoning the crocodile. They sat Sanzill up and listened quietly as he spoke.

"I am sorry, but as you all can see, I am not sure I can lead us anymore".

At first, Zao and Mao murmured but later kept quiet when they realized that even Zill had said no word. They wondered who would be the next leader of the trip and how the leader would lead them to seeing the birds. The war was imminent and the sick Monrau could as well have died or even got healed from his disease.

"In light of this, I want you all to appreciate Averyi who has always been with me in tough times. He stands by me anytime, even on sleepless nights when others have slept".

"Thank you Averyi", each of them said and hugged

Averyi.

"Now you all have to follow him because I have delegated my power to him".

"And I am taking it this time", Averyi collected the bamboo compass from Sanzill and clutched it to his chest with his lips pouted. "This time, I am leading".

Since none of them was interested in the position as a result of death and the recent accident, they all accepted Averyi, as the leader. Zao, Mao, and Zill continued with the crocodile and yam while Averyi and Sanzill discussed. When they were done, they brought some potion of the yam and each crocodile lap to both Averyi and Sanzill. Everyone ate quietly until Averyi ordered that they should continue. As if they had heard the voice of the gods, everyone scampered to get ready. Sanzill now supported himself with a stick and always walked beside Averyi, as Averyi had always been beside him.

Averyi looked into the compass and saw a tiny bird far away.

"Let's take this way", Sanzill pointed and they

walked along the strip beside the stream. There they found a little elf seated on a mound of earth. Elves were known to be playful beings; they believed he must have strayed from the other herds while playing. Averyi gesture that everyone should keep quiet. He made them stop at a spot and instructed Zill who knew how to sneak the best to go catch him. Elves might be playful but they hardly let down their guard, and they screamed a lot. So, Averyi and his troop members knew that they had to be extra-cautious.

They watched on as Zill sneaked toward the little elf. When he was close enough, he held the elf's mouth and nose tightly rested his weight on him and carried him away. When Zill got to the midst of the troop members, he dropped the elf, concussing him and causing a loud thud on the earth.

"Is he dead?" Averyi asked.

"No, I just concussed him", Zill replied. "He'll wake up in no time".

A few minutes later, the little elf coughed. He knew that they were enemies immediately, but there was nothing he could do about it. He was already in their custody, so he managed to put on a smile that would relax them a bit.

"Why is he laughing?" Zao asked.

"To his death. Who knows? Laughter could be their language of grief and fear when they're about to die". Averyi said and other members of the troop laughed. "Do you have any of your people around here?"

"No, I was playing hide-and-seek with my friends when I lost track of them".

"Oh, so do you want to see your friends?"

"Yes, I want to see them".

"My name is Averyi, I am a friend. I lead this team, and I can make you live if I so desire. I can also tell them to kill you if I want".

The elf rubbed his hands together and knelt. He looked like a mouse on the ground and amused Averyi so much he had to stifle the urge to laugh as the elf implored him to spare his life.

"I will spare you only if you can do me a little favor".

"What's the favor? I'll do it".

"Tell us where we can find Caladrius, the bird that heals".

"Caladrius? My father has the bird in his home right now".

A member of the troop gazed at the other with a loud surprise. Averyi raised the compass to his eyes and peeked through it. He saw the bird flying around in a dark room with its snow-white feathers illuminated. He nodded and faced other members of the troop.

"I think he is telling the truth, but there seem to be dangers ahead. I feel it".

"Well, we can't back off now that we've almost achieved what we came for. So we have to see what danger we want to trifle with".

"I see us overwhelmed by thick darkness in the shape of a dragon".

"So what are we doing about it? We let him go because there's danger ahead?" Sanzill asked, his eyes running from the elf to Averyi.

"No, there is a way we can go around it", Averyi said as he dug a hand into his pocket and brought out a gourd. He let out some powder on his palm, mixed it with saliva and abruptly stuffed it into the elf's mouth. The elf tried to prevent it but Averyi had already blocked his nose and mouth such that as he groped for breath, he swallowed the substance.

"What have you done to me?" the elf asked.

"It's nothing, I just poisoned you now. That's just a brief sport".

"Why not just kill me instead of this? Why not strangle me?"

"No, you aren't dead yet. I have the antidote. I'll give you time to go into the city and bring the bird here and when you come back, you get the antidote and go back in peace".

"Thank you, I'll be back now". He sprang on his feet and sped away, disappearing into the forest.

Averyi and his troop members laughed after the elf had gone. They loitered around waiting for the elf to arrive. After waiting for close to an hour, he emerged from the forest looking frail and with Caladrius, the snow white bird in hand. Averyi almost jumped with excitement when he saw the bird in the elf's hand. No sooner had the elf arrived than he collapsed at Averyi's feet. Averyi first seized the bird which cackled in his hand and passed it to Zill who held the legs and wings firmly.

Seeing that the elf was on the verge of losing his life, Averyi stuffed the elf's mouth with the antidote he had on him. As soon as the antidote dissolved in his mouth he sprang up and made to run toward the forest, but Sanzill hit the elf with the stick that supported his half leg and they both fell.

"Why did you do this?" Averyi asked with wild anger spreading over his face when he saw that the poor little elf's skull had been broken and blood gushed out. "I don't think killing him is needed".

Averyi heard heavy footsteps that sounded like falling massive pillars. He raised his head to look at the direction where the sound came from and saw a huge fire-breathing dragon with a huge head and six legs.

"Smok Wawelski!" Averyi screamed the name of the dragon and shouted, "run!" Everyone scampered. Averyi tried to hold Sanzill's hand as he ran behind other members of the troop. But it was too late. The fire from the dragon first dazed him before it turned him to soot within the blinking of an eye.

Averyi looked back and saw Sanzill dying in pain, but what could he have done? He caused this on himself, he shouldn't have killed the innocent elf. Different thoughts were running through his mind simultaneously that he didn't notice the dragon was already moving in his direction. He had been told about the story of a Smok Wawelski, he knows how evil and destructive the dragon is. He wasn't going to take a chance, if not for the fact that many great hunters powerful than him have tried and failed, then it's for the sake of Monrau's life, he has the Caladrius already. He ran as fast as he could.

The Journey Back

The team has been separated already, Mao, Zao and Zill were all together while Averyi was alone. Zao was scared and said to Mao, "I hope Averyi is somewhere safe with the bird, if anything happens to him, then we can't go back and face the people without the bird". Zill told them he saw Averyi waiting behind, "he must have been so stupid if he had thought of fighting the Smok Wawelski, let's just hope he didn't try to kill the dragon", he said.

Averyi just crossed a river and decided to take a short rest before continuing the journey, he sat and rested his back on a tree. It was dark already, he has to take a rest and continue the journey the following day. He looked for leaves and tied them together to make a virtual nest so that he could keep the bird inside to prevent it from escaping. The bird looked stressed from too much pressure applied on it, so Averyi was trying as much as possible not to suffocate the bird. He laid carefully and kept the bird very close to him.

It was dawn, Averyi rose up and picked up the bird, he continued his journey. Suddenly, he saw a glimpse of something that ran through the bush, he became scared and started shivering. "What could that have been?", he said to himself. He started walking carefully towards the direction he saw the frightening creature. "Did I really see something?", he started soliloquizing, "or was I just hallucinating?", those were the things running through his mind. He does not have enough time to waste, he has to keep moving.

Mao, Zao, and Zill were still together, they just woke up and were very hungry. "If we could walk down through this valley, we would see some trees with fruit", says Zill. They started walking down till they finally found a lot of trees with fruits on them. They started plucking and eating the fruits, they were eating as much as they could because they don't know the next time they will get to see food again before they make it out of the forest. "I need to ease myself, I am pressed" Zao said, Zill told him "you can use the bush, but don't go far and don't stay too long as well, we don't have too much time", "No problem, I will be fast" Zao replied. Zao started walking inside the bush to get a comfortable place to ease himself, he was going too far. He finally found a place and eased himself, it's now time to go back, he couldn't figure the road back. He tried remembering but just couldn't get it.

Mao and Zill had finished eating and slept off in the process. When they woke up, Zao still hadn't been back", Why is he taking too long? I thought you told him not to go far" said Mao, "I definitely did, what could have happened? We need to go and check him", replied Mill. "We can't afford to waste any more time, we need to leave here, we can't go back to look for him.

Zao still couldn't find a way back to where Mao and Zill were, then a howling sound came, he was frightened and couldn't control his emotions. He was scared and didn't know where the sound came from not to talk of knowing which direction to run. Suddenly, he saw a big creature moving towards his direction. He was so shocked and frightened that he couldn't move his legs till the violet creature feasted on him. That was the end of Zao.

They decided to look for Zao, they started the search, they went through the path he followed, they searched everywhere for him, they didn't see any sign of a human being. They refused to give up, they kept searching. "Mao!!!" Zill shouted, "I have seen something" he said, Mao was anxiously running to meet Zill. As he got there, Zill showed him Zao's empty skull which was dangling on the floor. Mao was very sad as well as frightened as well, he couldn't contain his shock. "We have to keep going", Zill said. They continue their journey back to the city.

They kept trying to find their way out of the forest, they couldn't exactly figure out the way they passed while coming, both of them seemed confused but they were trying their luck by guessing every time they are in the middle of one or two road paths. "The compass is with Averyi, he is the only one that knows the right path" Zao was lamenting, "Are we going to die in the forest now" asked Mill who was already scared. "we can't just sit here and die, we will try our best" Zao said. They kept going as Zao suggested. Suddenly, they can see a river from a distance. As they approached the river, Zao asked "Is this not the river where a crocodile attacked Sanzill?", they are back to where they were coming from. Then Zao noticed some heavy footsteps that sounded like falling massive pillars. He raised his head to look at the direction where the sound came from and saw a huge fire-breathing dragon with a huge head and six legs. Before they could move an inch, the fire from the dragon first dazed them before it turned them to soot within the blinking of an eye.

Averyi was still on the way back to the city, he had been through a lot, he hadn't eaten for two days. His legs are weakened, he can hardly move them. He felt tired but he kept going, hoping to meet Monrau alive in the city. He couldn't keep going any longer, he had to take a rest, so he sat and rested before continuing his journey. He saw a bushrat running just beside him, he ran after it, killed it. He roasted and ate it. He slept overnight in the forest, he kept the caladrius bird carefully beside him.

It was Daybreak, Averyi rose to continue on his journey back to the city, he took the caladrius bird and kept it in his pocket. He kept walking alone inside the forest with a brave heart despite being considered the laziest and most fearful soldier. He checked the compass which indicated that he should go towards his west, he complied and kept walking.

After 5 hours of walking, he saw a familiar footpath almost ten meters ahead, he couldn't vividly remember if they had come across the footpath but he was sure the footpath looked familiar. With a glimpse of hope, he walked towards the footpath. He started walking with a stressed looking face, he hasn't taken his bath in two days. He kept walking when he accidentally stepped on a snail, he looked down and wasn't even so concerned whatsoever. He continued walking, it looks like he is starting to have a bit of assurance and confidence.

"Yes!!!", Averyi shouted he had finally reached dry land. The joy in him can be felt by the whistling birds. He approached the city as he was smiling.

"Where are others?" one of the girls said as she saw

Averyi approaching from a distance, the second girl replied to her "do you expect all them to come back alive? " I just hope he has the caladrius bird with him"

"Averyi is back!!!", one of the soldiers shouted. Averyi's father came out and watched as his son walked in from the gate. "Were you able to get the Caladrius bird my son?" asked Averyi's father, Averyi then carefully brought out the bird from his pocket. "I was able to get the bird but I don't know the whereabouts of the other soldiers, Sanzill was killed by a Smok Wawelski, others might probably have died by now", Averyi said with tears on rolling down his eyes. "Well done my son let's go inside and see the King", they both entered the house. On getting inside, Averyi saw the King and was very sad, he could not control his emotions, the King can hardly move his leg, he was already bedridden. Averyi's father placed the Bird close to the King and recited some incantations, he then went outside to release the bird.

The King was given enough time to rest, "he will soon get better, tell the other soldiers the king will soon be fine", Averyi's father said, Averyi replied "okay father, thank you very much". Averyi went to meet the Commander and said to him, "the King will soon be fine, just give him time to rest", "alright, but we don't have enough time on our side, we have to move in a few days" the commander told Averyi.

The best strategy was a quick and immediate attack. The land of the Visors was far away, but they could reach it in three days, riding quickly. The wizards were locked in their castle, where they studied new spells and evil arts, their strength was not the art of war, but the use of magic and the evocation of monsters. They had to defeat them and then kill all the wizards to win the war, and it wouldn't have been easy. The Visors were not stupid enough to get them to the castle without any trap, and they had to provide constant supplies and medical care to the whole army.

The commander was impatient to leave as he was scared of being caught unaware, but everyone knew that it would not be possible to do it immediately. It took time, and to make sure that they were on the best, safest, and fastest path.

Averyi went back inside to stay with the king, the King was still sleeping, he decided to take a short nap as well, he hasn't slept for two days, his eyes are swollen already, he rested his back on the wall while trying to be vigilant as well. He slept off almost immediately.

It was dawn, Averyi yawned and stood up to check the king, he couldn't believe he completely slept off, he saw that the king was still sleeping. He was worried as he was expecting the king to be fine by now already. He went to the inner room to see his father, "Father wake up, the king is still unconscious, he should be fine by now", "the bird hasn't been completely healed, the king can't be healed immediately, it takes up to two to three days, you just have to be patient.

"The soldiers are already getting nervous, we are running out of time", said the commander, he was talking to Averyi, "I understand what you are talking about, but we can't go to war without the King" replied Averyi, he continued "The king will soon be okay, he just needs some time to regain his consciousness, all I need you to do for me is to talk to the other soldiers and let them know the king will be fine very soon".

Some of the city elders came around to see the king, they heard that they have found a way to heal Monrau. One of the guards took them to the where Monrau was, they entered and saw the King's condition, they were hoping to see the King been healed. "There is no change in the condition of the king, it's still the same like the same way we left him 3 days ago", a short man with a fully-grown beard said, the other elders were shocked as well. "Where is the native doctor that was called to take care of the king?" another elder asked. One of the king's guards was asked to call the native doctor, i.e., Averyi's father. Averyi's father came out and told the elders "I greet you all, the king has been treated, No one on earth in the air on the water can cure this illness. We would have been considering dumping him in some water if not for the existence of Caladrius… that's the snow-white bird, let me tell you a little tale about the bird", Averyi's father said. "This bird doesn't look at someone who is sick. The bird could heal a sick individual after it had taken all the illnesses on anyone. Once the bird takes the illness on itself, it spreads it to space so it could disappear. In the process, he would cure himself of the illness too, so Averyi and four other soldiers have gone to look for the Caladrius bird and luckily for us, they found it but only Averyi came back alive, the rest have died in the forest", he continued "we have done the required things with the bird and it has been released to spreads the sickness into space by healing itself, so the King will be fine, he just needs to rest a bit".

The elders were a little bit assured, they thanked the native doctor and went on their way back to their various houses. It's already getting dark, Averyi is back again to stay with the king overnight, he had previously gone to his house to have a proper bath and change his clothes.

Averyi's father went to where his King was lying, he recited some incantations, he sprinkled some herbs on the King's face, he was trying to make the king heal faster as he is under pressure to make things happen.

"I have not seen any significant change in the

health of the king since you used the Caladrius bird, how long do we still have to wait? I am tired of telling the soldiers story every now and then", Averyi asked his father, "don't worry, I have tried to hasten his healing process by reciting some incantations and giving him little herbs to drink", his father replied, he continued " I need to go and rest, I have a meeting to attend with other native doctors from other cities".

Averyi's father went into the inner room, while Averyi stayed with the king, he didn't want to rest his head because he did not want to sleep off, so he decided to stand and watch the King. It was midnight already, he was tired and feeling sleepy already, he had to sit and take a short nap. He could not withstand the cold breeze coming in from the window, less than two minutes that he sat on the chair, he slept off, with his legs on top of each other.

"Averyi! Averyi!! Averyi!!!" someone with a thick voice kept calling, Averyi could feel a hand tapping him continuously, he thought he was in the dreamland. He felt a heavier touch that he has been feeling earlier, he opened his eyes and couldn't believe what he saw, "the king is awake!!!" Averyi shouted, the guards entered, they were surprised and happy at the same time, they greeted Monrau.

"Is everyone ready for the war?" Monrau asked, Averyi replied "everyone is ready, we just need you before we go to war, we can't leave without you". "Okay, no problem, I am fine now, can you tell me about everything that happened in the forest?" Monrau asked, Averyi told him about what happened, how Sanchill got bitten by a crocodile and how they found the Caladrius bird used in healing him, he went ahead to explain how Sanchill killed the elf that helped get the Caladrius bird. Monrau was very sad and annoyed with Sanchill's decision to kill the elf, "how could he have done that? That's senseless and wicked", he continued "we can't just go to war against the Visors and the elves as well, we have to try and convince the elves to be on our side not to be against us".

"I have to go on a journey to appease the leaders of the Elves", Monrau said, Averyi's father entered upon hearing the voice of Monrau, he was happy to see that Monrau is now fine and now talking again. "I am glad you are fine once again Monrau", Averyi's father said, he continued "I have to leave now", Monrau replied "I have to thank you, I am grateful to you for saving my life, I would have been dead by now if not for you and our ancestors, I really appreciate, I will tell the guards to package some things for you, they will see you off and make sure you are safe before they turn back". "Ohhhh… thank you too, we should give thanks to our ancestors" Averyi's father said. Monrau signaled to the guards to pack some things for Averyi's father and see him off.

Monrau called a meeting of the Elders, he had asked one of the guards to pass the message to them. He went back to his room to wait for them. The elders came around in less than an hour.

"We are glad to see that you are now healthy and fine, we were here last evening and we were told by the native doctor that you will soon be fine, we are now happy you are fine" one of the Elders said, Monrau replied "I thank you all for everything you did, for your concern and care, I really appreciate, now that I am fine, we can't forget our first mission", he continued "that's why I called this meeting. Elder Reni stood up. "It has been a part of our history to meet great evils from time to time. Our ancestors have always faced it headlong and we have been victorious. I say we take what good Eddard has said and march into the forest to hunt down this monster. Aye!" After a lot of chants and speeches in support of Elder Eddard's proposition, Elder Kent was next. "My brothers, my mother's sons. Today we have shown that we have not been quick to forget history and all the great achievements of our tribe. However, it is important that we tread carefully in this matter. An invasion of a tribe is not the same as the sudden appearance of magical creatures. The recent happenings have shown that something sinister is at play in our village. Now that Monrau is fine, we have to find a way to defeat the Visors".

"I was thinking of trying to convince the elves to be on our side", said Monrau, he then continued by saying " but it has proven more difficult because I heard one of our soldiers who went to look for the Caladrius bird that was used to heal me, killed an innocent elf that helped them get the Caladrius bird, it's not acceptable, we have to appease the elves and not allow a situation where we will be fighting against elves and the Visors, our chance to win the war is definitely going to drop drastically if we are going to war against the two of them".

Then Elder Kent said "you have spoken the truth, going to war against the two of them is very risky, but we don't have enough time for all this, we have wasted enough time already, we have to act fast so that we don't get attacked unaware. We should not forget that the Visors are preparing for the war as well, don't let us make them hit us again before we react, we have...".

Suddenly Elder Eddard interrupted him "we understand, but we still can't go to war unprepared, we have to do all the necessary preparations before putting our lives on the line. There is no point putting our lives at risk and still end up losing the War. Its uncalled for, the whole city is at the risk of been taken at slave if we lose this war. Our wives will be taken and our children will be kept as prisoners, we have to do everything possible to win this war, there is a lot at stake".

Elder Ceddy added to what Elder Eddard said". We

are not here to argue or shout on ourselves, we are here to bring head together and conclude on what to do".

Monrau replied, he continued by saying. "From what you have all said now, you all want us to get prepared and not risk our lives for nothing, I will have to go and appease the leaders of the elf's, if we can convince them to fight with us against the Visors, then our chance of winning will definitely be high, so I will go with two or three soldiers to go and see the elves. We have to talk to them and appease them, but it's proving more difficult because I heard that one of the soldiers that followed Averyi to look for the Caladrius bird, he killed an elf which they will definitely know he is from us, but I will try my best with them to let them know that we want them to fight by our side".

Elder Kent then said, "Monrau, you have said well, you can have our full support concerning the matter, but I think you should rest a bit, you can let someone else go instead of going yourself"., Monrau replied, I understand what you are talking about, but nevertheless I have to go there myself, the leaders of the elves won't reckon with any soldier I send or else they see me, that's when they will know we are actually serious about what we came to ask them so I will be going to see them myself".

"Now that you have decided to go yourself, no problem, we wish you all well and pray to our ancestors to bring you back safe, you will come back in good health, no harm shall befall you, our ancestors shall protect you", Elder Sed added".Thank you all, I appreciate everything you have done, I pray that our ancestors will not make all our efforts futile, we don't have time to waste, I have to choose three soldiers to join me so that we can be on our way as soon as possible", Monrau said, he added "I will be ending the meeting now, thank you all for coming for coming, I appreciate your concern and presence here today"

Monrau left the meeting and went to meet the commander, "I need you to arrange three strong and able men for me, I need them to follow me to the realms of the elf, I need those men immediately", the commander replied, "That's not a problem, I will get that done as soon as possible, but you have to do everything very fast, we are taking the risk of been hit unaware", " No problem, we will be fast about it, just get me, three soldiers, as I said earlier" Monrau told him and left to his room to prepare for the journey to the realm of the elves.

Monrau was changing his dress when Averyi entered, "I overheard you talking to the commander that you need three soldiers to join you to see the leaders of the elves", asked Averyi.

Monrau answered him, "that's true, I need three strong soldiers to follow me to the realm of the elves, we have to appease them, the elves won't be happy with us because of what Sanchill did to one of them who helped you get the Caladrius bird which was used to heal me".

Averyi then told him, "I am interested in going with you, give me the chance to defend our people once again, I want to follow you to the realm of the elves", "Hmmmmm… I understand, but you just came back a few days ago after looking for the Caladrius bird, I can't let you go out there again, the war is near when we will all have the chance to defend our people, just stay at home and look after them, I will soon be back, tell the commander to hasten, I don't want it to get dark before we move" Monrau instructed him.

Averyi told him "alright, no problem, I will go and deliver your message now, but make sure you stay safe out there".

"I have summoned you all here to tell you that a new war is coming up. Not the one with the Visors. It's with time". Said the commander

"Time?" some of the soldiers chorused at once.

"Yes, Time", the leader cleared his throat. "Time is running and we can't risk been attacked unaware, the Visors are aware of the intention of planning war against them, we are planning of convincing the elves to be our side instead of making more enemies, we can, and we want three soldiers that are willing to protect and follow Monrau. This is the only way we can have a better chance of winning. Remember that if we lose him, we're losing the war, and if we lose this war, you're likely losing your life as well, so we have to protect him"

"I'm going", a vast soldier stepped out with his thin

arms glued to his sides.

"I am willing to die protecting Monrau", another soldier stepped out. He was built and hairy.

About ten other soldiers stepped out after the two, confessing their willingness to die for Monrau. Everyone loves and respects Monrau, they will do anything to protect and keep him alive, he is their greatest asset. The platoon leader selected three out of the soldiers and told them to follow Averyi who would tell them everything they needed to know about the mission.

"This mission is going to make each of you forever a hero. It's a privilege and you must regard it as such. As you can see, many stepped out to help but only very few of you were chosen. So move on with the courage to win and we shall win!"

"We shall win! We shall win! We Shall Win" the soldiers chorused as they marched on towards the entrance to the barracks.

When they were about to reach the gate, the commander quieted the soldiers and told them that they were not going to die.

"The mission here is to get to follow and protect Monrau as he travels to the realms of the Elves. He is going there to appease the leaders of the Elves and make them join us to fight against the Visors".

"That's a very simple task then", one of the soldiers said.

"Simple", other soldiers chorused and nodded with a great desire.

"They are all ready, they are outside waiting for you", the commander told Monrau, "okay, no problem, I will be with them soon" he replied. After some minutes, Monrau came out fully dressed, all the soldiers were hailing him, he told them to calm down and told the three soldiers that were chosen by the commander to follow him inside, he wanted to have a very short chat with them before leaving, "I hope the commander and Averyi has told you about the mission?" he said, he continued "we are not going to fight anyone, we are going to meet with the leaders of the Elves, but on our way, if we find any obstruction or enemy, we will destroy them", "yes!!!" the three soldiers chorused with a sign of great enthusiasm in them. "Now, let's move" he ended the conversation.

They all left the barrack, they started moving towards the outskirts of the city. Many soldiers including Averyi escorted them only to wave them goodbye after reaching the entrance into the forest, "Stay safe Monrau, our ancestors will protect you", Averyi said, Monrau replied and said "Thank you, I owe you a lot", Monrau was about entering the forest when Averyi shouted "wait!!! I have something for you", Monrau turned back and asked why Averyi had called them back, he gave Monrau the compass that was given to him by his father, it will make them get to the realm of the Elves faster and easier, it's a guide to get to the Elves realm, "thank you, this will prove a lot helpful, we have to go now, it's about to get dark". They left them and started their journey to the elves realm.

They journeyed quietly through the paths that led them into the Silent Forest which was known for its cemetery silence. The trees had a lot of fruit on them and they were very tasty and cold. Monrau made himself and the three soldiers sit for a while to eat some fruit and drink from a silently flowing river before they continued the journey.

When they crossed a roaring river and to a forest where they heard a lot of birds singing, they knew that they had left Silent Forest but knew not the name of the new place. Seeing that many of them would have grown weak, Monrau decided to make everyone rest for a while. They rested for some minutes, "It's late already, we can just spend the night here and keep moving tomorrow, and it's about to rain as well, let's get some leaves to cover ourselves and lay on the floor" Monrau said, one of the soldiers went to get something they can use to cover themselves, they laid it on the floor while they slept, Monrau didn't sleep, he was watching over the rest.

The dawn of the next day met Monrau wide awake, part of which was because of the troubling thoughts that had formed continuously in his mind and another reason being that the forest was suspiciously quiet. Then he heard it. A sweet voice singing quietly as if trying to make him sleep. His eyes started to close and he began dreaming immediately.

The war was over already, they had defeated the Visors and had sent the magical evil creatures back to extinction. His father was smiling at him and telling him that he was proud of him, he smiled back and heard his mother calling out to him. He turned around and saw his mother running towards him screaming what was inaudible. What was she saying? He wondered why she was screaming. Then he heard it faintly. "RUN". Run from what or from who? He turned back to ask his father but it wasn't his father that he saw, it was an ugly, formless being looking dirty and smeared with paint all over baring its teeth at him. Get away from me!

He shouted back into consciousness. He was back beside the river in the silent river. He looked around and saw two of his men walking unconsciously towards the river. The Bokwus!!! The Bokwus was not supposed to exist. Bokwus was an evil spirit that stole the souls of fishermen by pushing them off their boats and taking the souls to his forest. Bewildered, Monrau ran towards his men, tackled the first one down and knocked him unconscious. He does the same to the second one and looks around for the third one. He was nowhere to be found, he had been drowned already. This must be the forest of the dead! They had to get out quickly before the singing started again. Monrau wasn't sure he could come out of the dream again if he fell asleep. Scooping water with his hands, he splashed on his men waking them up. They gathered their things and left quickly.

As they walked on, Monrau looked into the bamboo that Avyeri had given to him shortly before their departure. Through the hole, he saw the familiar twin pole which signifies the elves' territory afar off. They continued to journey towards the twin poles non-stop because they wanted to move as far as possible from the forest of the dead. Monrau had lost one man, he wasn't prepared to lose another. They got to the elven forest by nightfall and decided to rest and gain their strength after such a tedious journey before facing Daniz, the elf king.

While the others slept, Monrau pondered on the quest before him. "What if the elf king isn't appeased?, then there's the possibility that he and his loyal men turn captives". He shrugged off this thought and reconsidered the outcome. "The elves are great allies of men, they will understand". "After all, I faced the Valkyries and survived " He thought again touching the scar on his back absentmindedly. Not long after this, Monrau, fell off to sleep.

The stabbing pain in his side woke him up, someone was hitting him with a spear end. At first, he panicked but as he began to grasp the situation, his tension eased. He looked around and saw his men were already in bondage surrounded by about ten elves each. Monrau, himself, was also being tied by a dozen elves. He could hear them whispering to each other; "he's strong, we have to keep him bound tightly". One thing was clear to Monrau, the elves feared him. All four men were blindfold and led into the presence of the elf king.

"Remove their blindfolds", commanded the elf king. The elves removed the blindfold from the eyes of Monrau and his men. "Monrau, it had always been a pleasure having you stop by until today. Quarim and 7 other elves were murdered gruesomely by your men and it was said that you ordered the killing of any elf that stands in the way of getting the healing bird". The elf king paused waiting for Monrau to make a comment.

"Great elven king Daniz, from the beginning you have been our ally and have always supported men right from time. Why would I pay you back this way for being kind to us? It is true that one of my men who was in quest of finding the healing bird to help me recover killed a little elf foolishly. However, I did not command such as I was barely alive myself and only one elf was killed. This is not to say that the crime isn't punishable but I will like you to be appeased and forgive my man's foolishness as he was also killed by the evil dragon unleashed by the visors. The diviners have decided to take revenge on us all and destroy everyone, this is the second reason why I have come to you today, that you and your followers fight with us against them and restore peace upon the Earth".

"What made you think you could sweet talk me into fighting alongside you murderers against the visors. As far as I am concerned, you and your men are my enemies and so you must all die to set things right. The visors are not the evil ones, you are!" The king Daniz thundered. "Take them to the death Forest and kill them all, I don't want their filthy blood on this land" the elf king commanded. With this, Monrau and his men were blindfolded again and bundled out of the throne room.

As Monrau and his men were being dragged out of the elf shelter, stones were being hurled at them. Monrau knew something wasn't right. The elves were known to men as jovial and funny; something is wrong with the elves. Panic thoughts gripped Monrau as they moved through the elf territory. "There is war ahead, if I die now my people will all die because they depend on me to lead them to war". "My ghost will not rest if I die without liberating my people". "What shall I tell my ancestors when I meet them after death?" "If only I hadn't slept... Monrau's thoughts paused. He heard something. " A cry! A cry that sounded like a woman's, a war cry. The Valkyries can't be here, are they? Am I imagining...

Just then, a war cry was heard from far again. This time, the elves paused and stood alert. They were puzzled as to if they should feel threatened or just move on with their mission. Another cry was heard again, this time it echoed around the forest. "Surely, it is the Valkyries" Monrau concluded undoubtedly. The Valkyries were known to instill fear in their opponents as a war strategy. They do this when they have the intention of not killing the opponents. It was just to create enough panic and confusion.

Just as intended, panic had grown among the elves present in the forest not seeing what was unto them. It all happened like a blur, a minute later the elves were down and unconscious by the hands of the Valkyries while Monrau and his men were liberated. Their blindfolds were removed and their bonds loosened.

"Asya" Monrau said with a bow acknowledging the Valkyries ruler. "thank you for freeing us, I must say that I wasn't expecting a rescue party but I am indebted by this, my lady" Monrau continued still bowing".

"Rise, Monrau. I did not forget what the evil spirit sent by the visors said. Remember, it was said that the elves and the dwarfs have been influenced by dark magic which means that whatever the elves do isn't of their own accord. I need to see the elf king so I can touch him with the wood from the Miller tree, this will inflict enough pain that will free him of the darkness that is controlling him. If we can do this, the other elves too will be free from the dark influence". Asya replied.

"In that case, let us go back to the elf kingdom. But how do we get to the king without being noticed?" Monrau asked. "That's simple, I have always wanted to use my acting skills in battle…

"That is interesting", Monrau said, looking amused by what he had heard. Never had he imagined that this killer Valkyries queen had a sense of humor.

"Bound them all!!!" Asya commanded.

A few minutes later, the Valkyries walked into the elf throne room carrying the unconscious elves on their shoulder and leading bound Monrau and his men to the king.

"What is this?! Thundered, elf king. "My king, the Valkyries have helped us to capture these murderers once again. They succeeded in killing our brothers but did not get far, thanks to the Valkyries who were passing by" Kansas, the chief elf guard replied. "Is that true?" Elven king asked, turning to Asya.

"Greetings, Daniz. My women and I found these ones while passing by the Kwalan forest. We found them planning their escape after killing your elves. I knew this Monrau was evil right from time (she hits Monrau with the Miller stick) when he came to me to war with them against the Visors. He's nothing like his father, he's a weakling and I desire nothing with him(she hits Monrau again with the Miller stick, he writhes in pain).

King Daniz roared with laughter hearing Monrau thrash around. "Oh Monrau, you went to the Valkyries for help? Serves you right. What is that stick? I see it is magical and I like that Monrau is being tortured, may I hit him with that stick too perhaps?" Daniz asked in amusement.

"Of course, king Daniz. You may". Asya said, smiling like a Cheshire cat. Asya walked gingerly to the throne to give Daniz the stick from the Miller tree. As she approached, Daniz stretched out his hand to receive it.

"I've never doubted my hidden talent for once", Asya said. "What do you mean, my lady?"

"This". With that, Asya evaded the outstretched King's hand and touched him with the end of the stick on the neck. Quickly, the Valkyries rounded up the remaining elves in the throne room choking them unconscious. Asya covered the mouth of king Daniz to muffle the scream and dropped him as he collapsed to the floor. Immediately, the same dark cloud that came out from Kobbs the elf's mouth came out of Daniz's mouth. "Asya, Asya. I'd always known women were cunning, you are brilliant but you test me too much and you shall die soon" the figure formed by the dark cloud screeched with laughter. The laughter echoed around the elven kingdom as all the elves in the kingdom convulsed the same dark cloud as their king.

"We shall see who dies first, I or Aldair your master. Tell him he's mine in the war" Asya spat out in anger. The smoke accumulated into one whirlwind form and whirled off the elven kingdom.

"Did you get it?" Asya asked, turning to Monrau.

"Yes, I did", Monrau said holding a small tubular translucent container which had a potion of the dark cloud in it dancing around as if trying to get out. Monrau and his men were not bonded tightly. So, while the cloudy figure was talking to Asya, he had captured part of the smoke in the container. "What about the rest of you?" Asya asked the Valkyries and Monrau's men. "We have it!" they chorused and held up similar tubes like Monrau's.

Just then, the elves and the king started to regain consciousness. Still weak from the effect of the Miller stick, the elven king asked painfully; "Why does my head ache?".

"Rest, Daniz. We will explain it all to you when you have enough strength to take it in". Asya hushed.

Tarasque

Meanwhile, back in Monrau's village, another mysterious creature had appeared. The tarasque was an extinct creature that was known to be a terror. The Tarasque was entirely covered with large, hard iron-like scales and had the head of a lion, six short legs, spikes all along its back and a scorpion's tail. This gruesome beast was said to have been the child of the mighty sea monster Leviathan. It could spew fire from its mouth and destroy buildings easily with a quick whip of its powerful and poisonous tail.

Sabil, the wife of elder Eddard was returning from gathering nuts when she heard a rustle behind her. She turned and beheld the six-legged evil. She didn't even get to scream before the beast turned her to ashes with the fire from its mouth.

Maloba, the ruler's messenger who had gone to see

the woman of his heart, got grazed by the beast's poisonous tail and barely got to the ruler's house to give the tale of the menacing beast before he gave up the ghost.

Immediately Maloba gave the news of the tarasque, a meeting was called by elder Eddard, the one who his wife got roasted to a crisp by the tarasque. With his head hung in sorrow, he asked, "what shall we do now that the chief isn't around? We cannot sit and watch while our loved ones are being killed, we have to do something! We have to fight this beast now!" "Elder Eddard, we understand your pain and how you feel about your wife's death. But we cannot just confront a mythical creature like this. You have spoken out of loss and have not considered the repercussion of fighting these evil creatures. They don't die easily, we have to destroy the wielder of the dark magic that brought them into existence". Replied Elder Kent.

"Rightly said, Elder Kent. We have to wait for the chief and the Valkyries who went as back up, to return before we can take any action. Besides, hasty decisions like the one you just suggested will cost lives that won't ever be regained. Please, let us all stay in our home and pray for the safe return of our leader and the Valkyries and hopefully the elves too if they agree to fight with us against the Visors". Elder Reni advised.

"That is all you have to say to me?" Elder Eddard shouted. "I will not rest till I kill the evil creature that killed my Sabil" Eddard said rushing out of the meeting hall. That was the last that was heard of the grief-stricken elder.

Avery's father returns...

Averyi was training with the other soldiers when the message came to him that his father sought after him. Perplexed, Averyi thought, "why would my father come back here, he had just left after helping to heal their chief. Is something wrong?". He quickly sheathed his sword and made his way to the waiting room for soldiers' visitors. "Father", Averyi bowed as he saw his father. "What brings you back here? I thought that you would have gotten back to your shelter by now, tell me, is anything wrong?.

"Ha, Averyi my son, nothing is wrong. I have decided to join the war against the Visors in my own little way. While I was traveling back, I felt the strong presence of a Kwalani, an evil spirit that possesses people and makes them do things unseemly. I suspect the wielder to be Aldair, Aldair is a powerful wizard and none of you stand a chance against him. I can bring him down. This is why I have come back, my son. If you, my once timid son can bring back the Caladrius, then I can bring down Aldair the wizard".

"Father, this is great. The chief would be glad to hear this, but he is currently on the quest to ask the elven king to join the war. Please abide in my house while we all await the chief's return". Averyi replied. Together, they both went to Avery's hut to discuss further.

The elves join the war!...

Daniz, the elven king recovered some hours later after he had been freed from the influence of the demon. He sat in the throne room with Asya and Monrau bidding them explain what had happened. The last thing the elven king remembered was going to bed fourteen days ago. Monrau started "Fourteen days ago must have been when you got possessed by the evil. The Visors have unleashed terror in the land, a lot of evil creatures have been released by the diviners to avenge the dark Shimir. I had requested earlier for a meeting with you but you declined as a result of the possession. Right now, we are at war and we need your help to win. Please fight with us to put an end to this evil. We are running out of time, The Visors want us all dead and they are already achieving that. What do you say, Daniz?"

"The Visors dare to take away the lives of the elves and you expect me to decline? Not while I live will the Visors thrive. I will lead my people to fight the war alongside Your people and the Valkyries. We will fight till our last strength to stop these evil diviners, I swear on the grave of all the brave elven Kings that I will protect my people from any danger. We will join you immediately Monrau, son of Biggis " "We shall also fight alongside brave Asya and the Valkyries to bring harmony and unity back to earth.

"Thank you, Daniz. You don't know how much this means to us all to have you fight with us. We shall journey tomorrow back to my land if that is fine by you so that we can prepare for war".

"Of course, I, the elders and the soldiers will journey back with you tomorrow"

"You have spoken well, Daniz. We also will fight alongside the elves to stop the evil Visors". Said Asya firmly.

By the dawn of the next day, Monrau and his men, Asya and the Valkyries and Daniz's army journeyed back to the land of Zorostars.

The arrival of the army...

"They are back with the elves!" The people of Zorostars whispered to each other excitedly. The previous days have been sad for the Zorostars as more people had been killed by the tarasque although it was minimized as a result of the Talisman prepared by Avery's father to protect them from the beast. The return of their chief with an army was a piece of mood-lifting news after all that had happened. The children, not used to seeing so many elves around stared in awe of the sight of the elven army.

"The soldiers led by Averyi who had gained respect

since he brought back the Caladrius rushed out to welcome their chief and counterparts into the land. A few hours later after everyone had rested, a meeting was called at the hall so that rulers, elders and high-rank soldiers could discuss the war Strategies. The people present at the meeting were Monrau, elders of Zorostars who were originally five but now four because of the death of Eddard, Avery, Avery's father, Kaiser, Macon, Rafal from the Zorostars soldiers were also present. Asya, the Valkyries queen, Fillis, kanya, Maine and Rasel from the Valkyries represented their clan. Daniz the elven king, Sacho, Alaris, Kansas, and Refal represented the elves.

As soon as everybody was seated, Monrau spoke; "Ladies and gentlemen…

"You forgot the elves", Daniz cut in jokingly.

Everyone laughed. "My sincere apologies Daniz. Ladies, gentlemen and elves...

Everybody laughed again.

Monrau continued, "We are gathered here today in unity to discuss the war ahead of us. I must say this that although war is said to cause pain and loses it has brought us all together in one accord. This is not to say that war is good, if there was anything in my power that I could do to restore peace in our various clans without the war, I would have done it but right now, it seems that the only path to peace is war. So, we shall go to war against the Visors and fight for our peace and freedom. Let us discuss now, the way to defeat the Visors.

Asya, the Valkyries queen, looked around and started. "Greetings rulers, elders and soldiers, as we already know that a war has been declared and we are at one side of the battle with the Visors at the other. During our visit to the Elven kingdom, we were able to capture little parts of the dark cloud into small tubes in order to experiment with and find out what works against it. Do we have healers that can work on them?"

Averyi's father spoke up this time, "I greet you all and commend our efforts put into ending this chaos. I am a healer whose son is a soldier in the land of Zorostars. I came from my shelter which is far from here to help heal the chief. On my way back, I felt a strong presence of an evil power which I believe was wielded by Aldair, a powerful wizard that was taught by the same man that taught me. We were taught to use the charms for good but he turned his back against the teachings of the master. I believe I can work on the sample captured by the soldiers if I am allowed. And will also like to go to the war front with you to face Aldair as none of you stand a chance against him. Thank you all".

"Thank you, Aviram. We are all grateful to have you join this war and we will be glad if you stopped the wizard, it seems he is the one who unleashed the evil creatures too. Once he is destroyed, they will all disappear just as they came. Who else has something to say?

"Greetings to you all, we elves have magic that can counter the mystical creatures. Just in case they are set against us in battle, line the elves up against them. We will go against them. As for the dwarves who are still under the spell of the Visors, we might just know the right potion to have them freed". Daniz the elven king supplied.

"That would be great. When can you get this potion ready so that we can have the dwarves back on our side?"

Monrau asked. "It takes 7 hours to brew the potion" answered Daniz

"It takes four days to get to the dwarves and back. We want to go to war as soon as we can. Is there a way to beat that? " Monrau asked. Daniz replied smiling, "Like I said, elves are also magical creatures, we can get to the dwarfs' kingdom and back in two seconds".

"Brilliant, I suppose we can start brewing the potion now and then proceed to war quickly", Asya replied wishing they would skip all the talks and start fighting already.

"Yes please, what herbs do you need? I and the Zorostars soldiers know the land well, we will go and get it" Averyi said.

"Very well then, let's get to work now". Daniz replied.

"We will meet again and draw our battle plan when the dwarfs get here".

The meeting closed with that and everyone set out to do their part.

The Visors

One foot into the land of the Visors would send a chill down the visitor's spine. The land of Visors reeked of evil so much that one does need magical powers to decipher that. Skulls hung around the village like ornaments. As if that isn't bad enough, the Visors' land was located in the north where the cold was enough to freeze fire.

Aldair the wizard sat in front of an unnatural fire that was burning without fuel or woods. One would have expected that the wizard was an older man. But Aldair was an old man in a young man's body in the literal sense. Aldair had grown so old as a result of the use of dark magic that he could barely walk. One day, he had killed one of his apprentices for disobeying him and also transferred his soul into the young man's body so that he could be young again. So, anybody who knew Aldair 10 years ago would not recognize him now. Whenever Aldair

135

was in a foul mood, his apprentices knew better than to come near him because the last one who tried to calm him was turned into a pot in which Aldair used to brew his dark potions.

Today, his apprentices could not stay standing in his presence for the fear of his wrath because the Kwalani had brought bad news to him. The Valkyries queen had freed the elves from his influence. "How dare she free his prisoners? And Monrau isn't dead? The mystical creatures he had released to gather souls for him were also not turning up because of Aviram. Aviram, Aviram!! That stupid half witted Aviram who was the other apprentice of Old Karim. Killing the old man had felt liberating, killing Aviram would give him more satisfaction after all the stupid old man loved the stupid Aviram more".

"Mmmaste-rr, the counc-il off eldd-err-s seek y-yyou" A trembling, frightened apprentice stammered. He was clearly aware of the calamity that might befall him.

"Ha, the council of elders. Come closer, are you scared? Don't worry I won't kill you" Aldair said to the trembling servant smiling. Still trembling, the servant moved towards him fearfully. "Do you happen to know the story of the cute little lamb?. Come closer and I shall tell it to you".

"One day the little lamb left its family because it wanted to be like the bear. It went to the bear's den and called out. Bear oh bear, I have come that you may teach me to have claws and strong teeth so I can protect my family. "Come closer, that I may teach you little lamb" the moment the lamb got to the bear, it tore it apart and feasted on it". The apprentice stared wide-eyed knowing that he had reached his end. "You see, I hate fragile little things like flowers, doves, eggs and you". With that he snapped his finger and the apprentice turned into a Small rock. "Now, you are strong, I will keep you as a pet". The wizard said laughing wickedly.

"Now, how do I explain my failure to the council of elders?" he thought, his smile had disappeared now. "I am so killing Aviram, the stupid Valkyries and arrogant Monrau.

The council of elders...

Five chairs sat at the extreme of the large room.

The room looks like a meeting hall but the commoners' chairs were dusty and rusty from lack of use. 7 years ago, when the original rulers of Visors were still alive, a prophecy had come forth. "Five shall rise from the descendants of the worshipers of the dark mistress and seek revenge on behalf of Shimir". When the elders of the land heard, they started to kill the descendants of the five diviners-; Shikam, Solarim, Goangi, Rakalh and fidopie. There had been only one left of each diviner's descendants, at their execution Aldair had mysteriously appeared and had collected the souls of all but a few young men who were left to serve. He had told the five that it was indeed their destiny to avenge Shimir. Now, the five sat on the chairs of the elders; Klaus, Rican, Binit, Claudius and Jamarius.

Aldair appeared in front of the five and bowed. "My Lords, you sent for me" Rican's thick voice vibrated on the walls and reverberated as he spoke. "Aladair, what is this that we have heard? The elves have been freed by Asya? Monrau is still alive and the number of souls being gathered is stagnant. I want to hear you say it yourself. Is it true that which we have heard?

"Unfortunately, Yes my Lords. It is as you have heard, but we have made progress here too, the souls of the Visors that were harvested are ready for battle, I assure you that even with the help of the Valkyries and the elves the Zorostars cannot win. The dwarfs are not going to join in, I made sure of that. We are stronger than they all are combined, my Lords.

"Hmmmm, what about the Bokwus, I heard that you could not control that spirit. Can you control it now? All the souls that it had gathered are not here, which means the Bokwus is storing them as its own. What have you got to say about that?" Jamarius said, frowning. "Lord Jamarius, I have finished the rites concerning that already. I shall call on the Bokwus now and it will answer and yield the harvested souls". "Show us" Binit demanded.

Aldair removed a potion sealed in a vial from his pocket and drank it. He shuddered violently and began to chant as soon as he recovered. The temperature in the room started to drop and the room became colder. A shapeless form materialized from thin air, it was the

Bokwus. "Yield your souls" Commanded Aldair sternly. As if being pulled by an unseen force, The Bokwus thrashed around for a while and yielded. Souls popped out of everywhere and stood behind Aldair. Pleased with these, Aldair said; "You see, my Lords. It is under control". Then to the Bokwus he said "Go and gather more souls, you better not fail me, you filthy creature!" The Bokwus looked menacingly at Aldair then disappeared just as it had come.

Aldair chanted again and all the soul disappeared. The temperature in the room suddenly became more conducive. "Well done, Aldair. This is good improvement" commended Klaus. "Now, you have to stop Monrau and his allies from winning. Unleash more chaos and make them run for their lives. I want then weak by the time we start the ritual for the awakening of the great dark goddess". Claudius said.

"Yes, my Lords I will not fail you again. The awakening will go smoothly and goddess Shmir will rule the souls of all men.

"Very well, you can leave now Aldair", Rican said.

Bowing again, Aldair paid homage to the five and disappeared.

The liberation of the dwarfs...

"What are you doing here, Daniz?" Kharis, the dwarf king asked. The elven king had appeared in the throne room of the dwarfs. "Why? To drink with an old friend. Have I crossed the line?" Daniz said feigning shock. "No, please come and sit with me, my friend. How long has it been now? 20 years?"

"18 years Kharis, age is beginning to tell on you. How have you been?"

"very fine"

Just then, a dwarf came in with two glasses of wine. Surprised, King Kharis asked; "how is it that you know that I have a visitor, cup bearer?" "I heard you talking and thought it would be appropriate to serve our visitor from far, some wine". "Good, I'm so thirsty from my journey, bring me a glass" Daniz said. The dwarf king collected the other glass of wine and took a sip. Almost immediately, he started to choke. "Kha-r-i—s...

"Relax my friend, soothed Daniz, I'm not killing you. I can't watch my friend being taken over by evil". The cupbearer transformed back to his normal elven self and shrugged. "Can't believe I was 4 feet shorter, so embarrassing" Drogo the elf king's son said. King Daniz coughed to choke back his laughter.

All around the dwarfs kingdom, the dark cloud was convulsed. The dwarfs were free from the dark influence too and without any persuasion agreed to join the war.

Preparation for war...

Not long after the arrival of the dwarfs, old men, women, and children were warned to stay indoors while the men, elves, dwarfs and the Valkyries prepared for war. Each soldier had bid their wives, children and old parents farewell because the war was about to start. In the council room, the leaders of each clan were there alongside high ranked soldiers of each clan.

"The elves will face the mystical creatures", Monrau said in conclusion.

"I guess nobody invites the Kobolds anymore...

Everyone turned towards the voice that had spoken. It belonged to Pierrot, the Kobolds leader. The Kobolds lived in the mines. They always warn miners in case of danger in the mines. They were like small dragons known for their trap building skills.

"Pierrot, my friend. I am sorry for not informing you but this is the season you hibernate. We couldn't find you in the mines. That was why you aren't here. All the same, we are glad you made it here. Your involvement is appreciated" Monrau said.

"We had earlier left to hibernate but one of us spotted a Smok Wawelski roaming the silent forest. I knew something wasn't right. We have come to help in whatever way we can. Wawoskis should be extinct.

"Thank you Pierrot, we are grateful to have you here. Kharis will go over the war plan with you while others go to prepare themselves for departure.

WAR!!!...

Monrau and the armies had arrived at the Visors territory. Everywhere seemed quiet. "where was the Visors clan? Is this a trap? Monrau thought, blood pumping in his ears. "Wait, I sense the dead here, plenty of souls that have been Bewitched" Avarim, said. Each leader signaled to their followers to halt. Suddenly, the atmosphere grew colder, dark souls started to form lines as though they were soldiers. "Impossible, we are fighting the dead? Dishonorable men. Asya spat.

That which is dead cannot die again. I'm afraid our weapons are ineffective against the souls. We need to destroy the wizard to stop them. All we can do now is hold them back to stop them from killing us". Avarim explained.

Monrau looked around and said, "Delegate power to your second in command, we are going to face the diviners and the wizard. Briefly, each ruler spoke to their delegates and charged them. Monrau then raised his sword and shouted: "To harmony!!!".

"To harmony!!" thundered the army and charged. Monrau, Asya, Daniz, Kharis, Pierrot, and Avarim made their way from the battlefront into the heart of the town. Skulls and Carcasses were scattered all over. Avarim stopped moving and pointed towards the mountain. "Over there! They are trying to awaken Shmir, they cannot be successful, Shmir is hatred herself, we have to stop them.

"Hold on, I will take us up", the elven king said. With a snap of his finger, the six of them were at the mountain top which was freezing. Avarim pointed and said. There they are!

"where was Aldair?" Avarim wondered. There were just five diviners and a young man about thirty. Meanwhile, the five leaders engaged the diviners. Avarim could feel Aldair's energy coming from the young man walking towards him. "Avarim, it will be my pleasure to finally end your life today", Avarim said smiling bitterly at Avarim.

"I see that you have gotten yourself a new body or shall I say, stolen a new body", Avarim said smiling. "How shall we do this then? I don't want to waste my magic on you and I've been dying to duel with this young body" Aldair said unsheathing his sword. "I will like to slice you to pieces for everything you have cost me. This body belonged to one of my apprentices who was a swordsman before I coerced him into serving me" Aldair boasted swinging the sword skillfully still walking towards Avarim. Avarim also unsheathed his sword. It happened like a blur, Avarim had allowed Aldair to think he'd really use the sword but had carefully picked up the vial that contained the sleeping smoke. The moment Avarim swung his sword, he had let go of the vial such that when it broke at Aldair's feet, the content enveloped him. Now on the ground, Aldair managed to say "You cheated..." Avarim looked down at him and laughed, "you were thinking I'd be fair with you after killing the master? Aldair was barely conscious.

Avarim knelt down beside Aldair and brought out his dagger. He sliced Aldair's arm enough to draw blood and carefully opened one of the vials that had the dark cloud inside and dripped blood inside it. For a while, it looked like a battle inside the vial but moments later, the smoke became something like vapor and cooled. At the war front, the dark souls suddenly went still and stopped fighting. One by one the darkness in the souls evaporated leaving them pure and harmless. Once the blood of the wielder has been fed to the Kwalani, it stops prevailing and ceases to serve the wielder. The mystical creatures also disappeared from the surface of the earth. Without many battles, the war had been won. The five rulers had overcome the diviners. Asya had killed the diviner she faced while the others had their opponents wounded at their feet.

The remaining four diviners and the wizard were bound. Before they left the Visors land, Avarim performed rites to give rest to the souls and applied the juice of the Miller leaf to Aldair's knife cut. The juice from the Miller leaf was said to render a magician impotent after it has been mixed with the magician's blood. The same thing was done for the four diviners too. The captives in Aldair's dungeon were rescued and taken to the Zorostars village.

All the clans returned to their territories victorious. Once again, peace had been restored upon the Earth.